ALL HE TAKES

(A Nicky Lyons FBI Suspense Thriller—Book Six)

BLAKE PIERCE

Blake Pierce

Blake Pierce is the USA Today bestselling author of the RILEY PAGE mystery series, which includes seventeen books. Blake Pierce is also the author of the MACKENZIE WHITE mystery series, comprising fourteen books; of the AVERY BLACK mystery series, comprising six books; of the KERI LOCKE mystery series, comprising five books; of the MAKING OF RILEY PAIGE mystery series, comprising six books; of the KATE WISE mystery series, comprising seven books; of the CHLOE FINE psychological suspense mystery, comprising six books; of the JESSIE HUNT psychological suspense thriller series, comprising twenty six books; of the AU PAIR psychological suspense thriller series, comprising three books; of the ZOE PRIME mystery series, comprising six books; of the ADELE SHARP mystery series, comprising sixteen books, of the EUROPEAN VOYAGE cozy mystery series, comprising six books; of the LAURA FROST FBI suspense thriller, comprising eleven books; of the ELLA DARK FBI suspense thriller, comprising fourteen books (and counting); of the A YEAR IN EUROPE cozy mystery series, comprising nine books, of the AVA GOLD mystery series, comprising six books; of the RACHEL GIFT mystery series, comprising ten books (and counting); of the VALERIE LAW mystery series, comprising nine books (and counting); of the PAIGE KING mystery series, comprising eight books (and counting); of the MAY MOORE mystery series, comprising eleven books (and counting); the CORA SHIELDS mystery series, comprising five books (and counting); of the NICKY LYONS mystery series, comprising seven books (and counting), of the CAMI LARK mystery series, comprising five books (and counting), of the AMBER YOUNG mystery series, comprising five books (and counting), of the DAISY FORTUNE mystery series, comprising five books (and counting), and of the new FIONA RED mystery series, comprising five books (and counting).

An avid reader and lifelong fan of the mystery and thriller genres, Blake loves to hear from you, so please feel free to visit www.blakepierceauthor.com to learn more and stay in touch.

Copyright © 2023 by Blake Pierce. All rights reserved. Except as permitted under the U.S. Copyright Act of 1976, no part of this publication may be reproduced, distributed or transmitted in any form or by any means, or stored in a database or retrieval system, without the prior permission of the author. This ebook is licensed for your personal enjoyment only. This ebook may not be re-sold or given away to other people. If you would like to share this book with another person, please purchase an additional copy for each recipient. If you're reading this book and did not purchase it, or it was not purchased for your use only, then please return it and purchase your own copy. Thank you for respecting the hard work of this author. This is

a work of fiction. Names, characters, businesses, organizations, places, events, and incidents either are the product of the author's imagination or are used fictionally. Any resemblance to actual persons, living or dead, is entirely coincidental. Jacket image Copyright Mr Dasenna used under license from Shutterstock.com.
ISBN: 978-1-0943-8102-2

BOOKS BY BLAKE PIERCE

FIONA RED MYSTERY SERIES
LET HER GO (Book #1)
LET HER BE (Book #2)
LET HER HOPE (Book #3)
LET HER WISH (Book #4)
LET HER LIVE (Book #5)

DAISY FORTUNE MYSTERY SERIES
NEED YOU (Book #1)
CLAIM YOU (Book #2)
CRAVE YOU (Book #3)
CHOOSE YOU (Book #4)
CHASE YOU (Book #5)

AMBER YOUNG MYSTERY SERIES
ABSENT PITY (Book #1)
ABSENT REMORSE (Book #2)
ABSENT FEELING (Book #3)
ABSENT MERCY (Book #4)
ABSENT REASON (Book #5)

CAMI LARK MYSTERY SERIES
JUST ME (Book #1)
JUST OUTSIDE (Book #2)
JUST RIGHT (Book #3)
JUST FORGET (Book #4)
JUST ONCE (Book #5)

NICKY LYONS MYSTERY SERIES
ALL MINE (Book #1)
ALL HIS (Book #2)
ALL HE SEES (Book #3)
ALL ALONE (Book #4)
ALL FOR ONE (Book #5)
ALL HE TAKES (Book #6)
ALL FOR ME (Book #7)

CORA SHIELDS MYSTERY SERIES

UNDONE (Book #1)
UNWANTED (Book #2)
UNHINGED (Book #3)
UNSAID (Book #4)
UNGLUED (Book #5)

MAY MOORE SUSPENSE THRILLER

NEVER RUN (Book #1)
NEVER TELL (Book #2)
NEVER LIVE (Book #3)
NEVER HIDE (Book #4)
NEVER FORGIVE (Book #5)
NEVER AGAIN (Book #6)
NEVER LOOK BACK (Book #7)
NEVER FORGET (Book #8)
NEVER LET GO (Book #9)
NEVER PRETEND (Book #10)
NEVER HESITATE (Book #11)

PAIGE KING MYSTERY SERIES

THE GIRL HE PINED (Book #1)
THE GIRL HE CHOSE (Book #2)
THE GIRL HE TOOK (Book #3)
THE GIRL HE WISHED (Book #4)
THE GIRL HE CROWNED (Book #5)
THE GIRL HE WATCHED (Book #6)
THE GIRL HE WANTED (Book #7)
THE GIRL HE CLAIMED (Book #8)

VALERIE LAW MYSTERY SERIES

NO MERCY (Book #1)
NO PITY (Book #2)
NO FEAR (Book #3)
NO SLEEP (Book #4)
NO QUARTER (Book #5)
NO CHANCE (Book #6)
NO REFUGE (Book #7)
NO GRACE (Book #8)
NO ESCAPE (Book #9)

RACHEL GIFT MYSTERY SERIES
HER LAST WISH (Book #1)
HER LAST CHANCE (Book #2)
HER LAST HOPE (Book #3)
HER LAST FEAR (Book #4)
HER LAST CHOICE (Book #5)
HER LAST BREATH (Book #6)
HER LAST MISTAKE (Book #7)
HER LAST DESIRE (Book #8)
HER LAST REGRET (Book #9)
HER LAST HOUR (Book #10)

AVA GOLD MYSTERY SERIES
CITY OF PREY (Book #1)
CITY OF FEAR (Book #2)
CITY OF BONES (Book #3)
CITY OF GHOSTS (Book #4)
CITY OF DEATH (Book #5)
CITY OF VICE (Book #6)

A YEAR IN EUROPE
A MURDER IN PARIS (Book #1)
DEATH IN FLORENCE (Book #2)
VENGEANCE IN VIENNA (Book #3)
A FATALITY IN SPAIN (Book #4)

ELLA DARK FBI SUSPENSE THRILLER
GIRL, ALONE (Book #1)
GIRL, TAKEN (Book #2)
GIRL, HUNTED (Book #3)
GIRL, SILENCED (Book #4)
GIRL, VANISHED (Book 5)
GIRL ERASED (Book #6)
GIRL, FORSAKEN (Book #7)
GIRL, TRAPPED (Book #8)
GIRL, EXPENDABLE (Book #9)
GIRL, ESCAPED (Book #10)
GIRL, HIS (Book #11)
GIRL, LURED (Book #12)
GIRL, MISSING (Book #13)
GIRL, UNKNOWN (Book #14)

LAURA FROST FBI SUSPENSE THRILLER

ALREADY GONE (Book #1)
ALREADY SEEN (Book #2)
ALREADY TRAPPED (Book #3)
ALREADY MISSING (Book #4)
ALREADY DEAD (Book #5)
ALREADY TAKEN (Book #6)
ALREADY CHOSEN (Book #7)
ALREADY LOST (Book #8)
ALREADY HIS (Book #9)
ALREADY LURED (Book #10)
ALREADY COLD (Book #11)

EUROPEAN VOYAGE COZY MYSTERY SERIES

MURDER (AND BAKLAVA) (Book #1)
DEATH (AND APPLE STRUDEL) (Book #2)
CRIME (AND LAGER) (Book #3)
MISFORTUNE (AND GOUDA) (Book #4)
CALAMITY (AND A DANISH) (Book #5)
MAYHEM (AND HERRING) (Book #6)

ADELE SHARP MYSTERY SERIES

LEFT TO DIE (Book #1)
LEFT TO RUN (Book #2)
LEFT TO HIDE (Book #3)
LEFT TO KILL (Book #4)
LEFT TO MURDER (Book #5)
LEFT TO ENVY (Book #6)
LEFT TO LAPSE (Book #7)
LEFT TO VANISH (Book #8)
LEFT TO HUNT (Book #9)
LEFT TO FEAR (Book #10)
LEFT TO PREY (Book #11)
LEFT TO LURE (Book #12)
LEFT TO CRAVE (Book #13)
LEFT TO LOATHE (Book #14)
LEFT TO HARM (Book #15)
LEFT TO RUIN (Book #16)

THE AU PAIR SERIES

ALMOST GONE (Book#1)
ALMOST LOST (Book #2)
ALMOST DEAD (Book #3)

ZOE PRIME MYSTERY SERIES
FACE OF DEATH (Book#1)
FACE OF MURDER (Book #2)
FACE OF FEAR (Book #3)
FACE OF MADNESS (Book #4)
FACE OF FURY (Book #5)
FACE OF DARKNESS (Book #6)

A JESSIE HUNT PSYCHOLOGICAL SUSPENSE SERIES
THE PERFECT WIFE (Book #1)
THE PERFECT BLOCK (Book #2)
THE PERFECT HOUSE (Book #3)
THE PERFECT SMILE (Book #4)
THE PERFECT LIE (Book #5)
THE PERFECT LOOK (Book #6)
THE PERFECT AFFAIR (Book #7)
THE PERFECT ALIBI (Book #8)
THE PERFECT NEIGHBOR (Book #9)
THE PERFECT DISGUISE (Book #10)
THE PERFECT SECRET (Book #11)
THE PERFECT FAÇADE (Book #12)
THE PERFECT IMPRESSION (Book #13)
THE PERFECT DECEIT (Book #14)
THE PERFECT MISTRESS (Book #15)
THE PERFECT IMAGE (Book #16)
THE PERFECT VEIL (Book #17)
THE PERFECT INDISCRETION (Book #18)
THE PERFECT RUMOR (Book #19)
THE PERFECT COUPLE (Book #20)
THE PERFECT MURDER (Book #21)
THE PERFECT HUSBAND (Book #22)
THE PERFECT SCANDAL (Book #23)
THE PERFECT MASK (Book #24)
THE PERFECT RUSE (Book #25)
THE PERFECT VENEER (Book #26)

CHLOE FINE PSYCHOLOGICAL SUSPENSE SERIES

NEXT DOOR (Book #1)
A NEIGHBOR'S LIE (Book #2)
CUL DE SAC (Book #3)
SILENT NEIGHBOR (Book #4)
HOMECOMING (Book #5)
TINTED WINDOWS (Book #6)

KATE WISE MYSTERY SERIES
IF SHE KNEW (Book #1)
IF SHE SAW (Book #2)
IF SHE RAN (Book #3)
IF SHE HID (Book #4)
IF SHE FLED (Book #5)
IF SHE FEARED (Book #6)
IF SHE HEARD (Book #7)

THE MAKING OF RILEY PAIGE SERIES
WATCHING (Book #1)
WAITING (Book #2)
LURING (Book #3)
TAKING (Book #4)
STALKING (Book #5)
KILLING (Book #6)

RILEY PAIGE MYSTERY SERIES
ONCE GONE (Book #1)
ONCE TAKEN (Book #2)
ONCE CRAVED (Book #3)
ONCE LURED (Book #4)
ONCE HUNTED (Book #5)
ONCE PINED (Book #6)
ONCE FORSAKEN (Book #7)
ONCE COLD (Book #8)
ONCE STALKED (Book #9)
ONCE LOST (Book #10)
ONCE BURIED (Book #11)
ONCE BOUND (Book #12)
ONCE TRAPPED (Book #13)
ONCE DORMANT (Book #14)
ONCE SHUNNED (Book #15)
ONCE MISSED (Book #16)

ONCE CHOSEN (Book #17)

MACKENZIE WHITE MYSTERY SERIES

BEFORE HE KILLS (Book #1)
BEFORE HE SEES (Book #2)
BEFORE HE COVETS (Book #3)
BEFORE HE TAKES (Book #4)
BEFORE HE NEEDS (Book #5)
BEFORE HE FEELS (Book #6)
BEFORE HE SINS (Book #7)
BEFORE HE HUNTS (Book #8)
BEFORE HE PREYS (Book #9)
BEFORE HE LONGS (Book #10)
BEFORE HE LAPSES (Book #11)
BEFORE HE ENVIES (Book #12)
BEFORE HE STALKS (Book #13)
BEFORE HE HARMS (Book #14)

AVERY BLACK MYSTERY SERIES

CAUSE TO KILL (Book #1)
CAUSE TO RUN (Book #2)
CAUSE TO HIDE (Book #3)
CAUSE TO FEAR (Book #4)
CAUSE TO SAVE (Book #5)
CAUSE TO DREAD (Book #6)

KERI LOCKE MYSTERY SERIES

A TRACE OF DEATH (Book #1)
A TRACE OF MURDER (Book #2)
A TRACE OF VICE (Book #3)
A TRACE OF CRIME (Book #4)
A TRACE OF HOPE (Book #5)

PROLOGUE

They say a photograph can capture the soul. That was what June Lockheart believed, anyway. As she made her way through the antique store, passing by rows upon rows of vintage clothing, she knew exactly where she was going: the camera section at the back. These days, this was one of the only places she could still see real Polaroid cameras.

And as she passed by the racks of dresses, she couldn't help but smile.

She was in her late twenties, and she'd been taking photographs for years. She was self-taught and had seen plenty of success with her work. She'd shot weddings, birthdays, anniversaries, engagements and even the odd wedding proposal. But it wasn't just her work that had been successful—it was also the people that she'd been photographing. She'd been showing some of her work around and had even managed to sell a few prints. That hadn't been enough for her, though. No, she wanted to do more with her work. She wanted to do something special. She wanted people to see that her work was worth something.

And that was why she was standing in this antique store, where she'd been hoping to find a Polaroid camera to work with. She'd been struggling to find a way to showcase her work properly. She wanted to find a way to take her photographs and make them special. And while she'd been looking, she'd also been thinking. She needed a real challenge. She needed something that would really stretch her as a photographer. She needed to prove that she could capture amazing, emotion-invoking photos, even with old technology.

That's the reason she was looking for a Polaroid camera. And now it was time to choose. She'd been through the aisles and it was time to settle.

She reached the back of the antique store, and as she did, she couldn't help but smile. There were so many cameras here. They stood on the shelves in front of her, cameras and lenses of all kinds and types. She reached out and grabbed a camera. It was one which had seen better days. It was old and the lens was scratched, but it was a beautiful camera that she could tell took good pictures.

But as she took a step closer, she noticed a small shelf that contained a pile of Polaroid photos. Someone must have brought them in! June couldn't resist her curiosity; she had to take a look, so she went over to the shelf and picked up the pile, then began to sift through them.

She grinned when she saw the first few photos. They were all of a young couple and the two were clearly very much in love. She could tell just by looking at the photos and their subjects that this was a couple that cared deeply for each other. As she looked further, she saw other photos of the same couple. They were all here, in the pile.

They had been taken at a variety of different places, and as June looked at each one, she could tell that they were from different periods in the couple's relationship. In one, the young man was holding his new wife close and the two were clearly very much in love. In another, the wife was holding her husband's hand as they walked through a field. June could tell that they were out on a picnic, just the two of them. The smiles on their faces were genuine and the two were clearly very much in love. June couldn't help but smile. These photos were beautiful.

She'd been taking photos for years. She'd taken photos of the same subjects on many different occasions, and she knew that people could tell a lot from photos. She could tell when a couple had been together for a long time. She could tell when a couple was in love.

But as June flipped through more photos, the subject matter changed. It shifted from old family photos, to portrait-style pictures of young women.

Then, she reached halfway through the stack, and a photo gave her pause.

It was a woman lying on a floor in a white dress.

But something wasn't right. There was red all over her dress, and--

June's blood froze over. In the photo... the woman's throat had been slit.

June could feel her heart beating in her ears. And she could feel her stomach turn over. She felt like she was about to throw up, and she couldn't believe what she was seeing. Her hands trembled as she reached for the next photo, and she felt her heart sink even further.

This had to be fake, right? But it looked so real, and her stomach was queasy. She had seen a lot of fake bodies in movies and all that, but this was different. The woman's eyes were glazed over in a way that looked so real.

Suddenly paranoid, June looked over her shoulder. Across the shop, she could see the store owner, a friendly old man, behind the counter, writing something down.

She didn't know who took this photo.

Maybe it was him.

Maybe it was someone else.

All she knew was that she needed to take this to the police.

CHAPTER ONE

Agent Nicky Lyons of the FBI sat in her car in the parking lot of the prison, watching from a distance, studying the tall gray walls and the barbed wire fences. It was morning, and the sun peeked over the back of the prison, bringing light and life to an otherwise drab, dreary scene.

She needed to get back in there. But she had to be tactful.

Inside that prison was Felix Anderson, a kidnapper who Nicky had put behind bars not that long ago. Felix also happened to be a deranged psychopath who had been leading her on with clues about her missing sister, Rosie. Nicky had been kidnapped with Rosie when they were teenagers by an unknown man.

Nicky escaped.

Rosie didn't.

And ever since then, now twenty-nine-year-old Nicky had dedicated her life to missing persons cases. There was one issue... she had never found her own sister, who Nicky believed was still out there somewhere.

Recently, and thanks to Felix, Nicky had been given a major hint. She suspected the kidnapper was someone who knew her father, back in West Virginia; but on top of that, the last time she saw Felix, she had finally gained the upper hand.

She'd tricked Felix into revealing a crucial detail about the kidnapper.

The kidnapper was someone who had mentored Felix. Nicky was sure of it, and Felix's reaction had confirmed her suspicions. He hadn't given up a name, but Nicky was damn sure he knew the identity of the kidnapper, and she had to find a way to make him talk.

Nicky looked down at her phone in the console of her car. She picked it up, smoothing her thumb along its surface.

It had only been two days since she'd talked to her father.

He'd called her. It was the most contact Nicky and her dad had in years. The man was a drunk, and was never a great father, but Nicky knew she might need him. She couldn't reveal anything about Felix, or about the potential kidnapper.

But sooner or later, she was going to have to go back to Nelly, West Virginia, and see her father... and see what he might know. While she felt confident in the theory that her father might have known the killer in real life, Nicky never suspected her father necessarily had anything to do with the kidnapping. That would be… unthinkable, really. Her dad had loved Rosie, more than he'd loved Nicky, and she couldn't imagine a world in which he'd let someone hurt her or get away with hurting her.

Then again, her dad did also become even more drunk and unhinged after Rosie's disappearance. Could guilt be a factor?

Nicky considered it, but it just didn't check out in her mind. No, it seemed more likely that the kidnapper could be someone her dad knew, even casually. A co-worker, a mechanic, someone who Nicky and Rosie had never seen before… but someone who could have seen them, stalked them…

After all, when he'd followed them home from the mall that day, it had seemed so deliberate. Maybe he did randomly choose them from the pick of teenage girls at the mall, but then again, it was possible he'd scoped them out.

Nicky just didn't know. There were so many unanswered questions—too many.

Taking a breath, Nicky faced the prison again. She'd been building her game plan up, but Felix was smart, and she didn't know if it would work. It had been hard enough for Nicky to get an inkling of information from Felix.

But maybe someone else could.

An informant.

Nicky was hoping she could bribe another inmate into cozying up to Felix and getting information. Open on her passenger seat was a file, and Nicky picked it up.

Fred Garrison. In for robbery. Only a year left on his term, and he'd had good behavior. Nicky looked at the mugshot of Fred, a gruff man with a scar down his face. His criminal rap sheet was surprisingly short, but he looked the part, with tattoos and all. However, there was one event in his past that had made him stand out to Nicky among the pool of potential candidates. During a robbery at the bank, Fred had kidnapped a woman and taken her hostage. Of course, Felix knew more than a few things about keeping women hostage, so maybe Fred could use this to relate to him.

Either way, Nicky doubted Felix would suspect a man like Fred would be an informant for the FBI.

Could he get the information she needed?

She hoped so.

Nicky grabbed the file, along with her handbag, and locked her car. She took a breath and headed toward the prison. The hot Florida sun beat down on her, but she pushed on.

It was time to meet Fred.

Inside, the prison was as dark and cold as it ever was. The guard, a man behind plexiglass, had grown used to seeing Nicky, and he nodded at her.

"Agent Lyons, I saw you scheduled something with us," he said.

"I did," Nicky replied.

"Good. I'll let them know you're here."

The guard radioed up to the prison, and before Nicky even had time to sit, the guard told her she could proceed. She opened the doors, passing through the metal detectors and getting patted down.

The guard led her down the long, imposing hallways of the prison, and Nicky was filled with a sense of dread. There was no guarantee that Fred would agree to this, or that he was trustworthy, but he seemed to be the best candidate.

Once they reached a door, the guard opened it for Nicky.

"Go right in. Garrison will be out shortly."

The door buzzed, and Nicky walked in. The visitation hall was small, with a few tables and chairs. A television was mounted on the wall, and there was a clear divider between the prisoners and the visitors. There was a single door on the other side of the divider; it opened, and Fred came out. He was a big man, with huge shoulders and a thick chin. His arms were covered in tattoos, and he had a scar across his face. His green eyes were piercing.

"Thank you," Nicky said to the guard. "I can take it from here."

"We'll be right outside if you need anything," the guard said.

With that, Nicky was left alone with Fred Garrison.

He eyed her up and down, as though trying to read her, and Nicky kept her own gaze firm.

"Mr. Garrison," she began. "Do you know why I'm here?"

"I have no idea," Fred said. "Are you some kind of therapist?"

Nicky shook her head. "I'm with the FBI. My name is Nicky Lyons."

"FBI?" He raised an eyebrow. "Shit, what is this about? They told me I'd been on good behavior."

"You aren't in trouble, Fred," Nicky said. "Actually, I was thinking you and I might be able to help each other."

Fred's eyes flashed. Nicky kept her posture strong.

"You've got my attention," Fred said. "What do you want, and what do I get out of it?"

Nicky cleared her throat and crossed her hands on the table. "Here's the thing, Fred. You only have a year left in this place. You've been good. The ideal inmate, actually. What if I told you I could get you out of here sooner?"

"I'd marry you," Fred said, but his expression was serious. "What's in it for you?"

"I need you to get some information for me," Nicky stated. "There's a man in this prison. Felix Anderson. He was arrested for kidnapping and believe me when I say that this is a twisted man. What I need is for you to get close to him and get a name for me."

"Sounds like a dangerous game."

"It is," Nicky said. "But if you do this for me, I can get you out of here in less than a year. I can get you a cushy job. I can get you out of Florida and away from here in general."

"Shit, I'd do anything to get out of this hellhole."

"Then let's do this," Nicky said. "I want you to get information on a kidnapper, someone who was Felix's mentor. You can ask Felix all the questions you want, but you need to do it in a way that doesn't make him suspicious. I want to know the name of the man who mentored Felix and taught him how to kidnap girls."

Fred leaned back in his chair. "And how the hell am I supposed to do that?"

"You become his friend. You stay close to him. Make up something about your past he might be able to relate to. Make yourself someone he can trust, then find out the information. All I need is the name of the person who mentored him. Even if it's just a first name, or just a last name--anything will help."

Fred stared at Nicky for a long time. She felt tense and nervous, but she kept her posture strong. She was ready to do whatever it took to save Rosie, and if it meant bribing a con in order to get information, then that's what she'd have to do.

Fred finally nodded. "I'll get the information for you."

Relief hit her. She got the immediate sense that Fred meant it--he had a sincerity in his eyes.

"Thank you, Fred," Nicky said.

"But for this to work, you have to get me out of here early. I do this for you, I want that deal."

"And I'll make sure you get it."

Nicky was about to stand when Fred began to say something else.

"You said he was kidnapping girls," Fred said. A certain emotion filled his eyes, and Nicky relaxed in her seat.

"Yes," she said. "He was kidnapping twin sisters and playing games with them, threatening to kill one if another tried to escape. But I was able to stop him. The person who mentored him seemed to have a similar fascination with sisters." Nicky left out the part where she knew, firsthand, what it felt like to be kidnapped by that man. She couldn't quite put into words the evil she'd experienced.

"I've got daughters waiting for me outside of this place," Fred said. "I'll get you the information."

Nicky nodded. She didn't know if Fred was the right person to get the information, but he seemed to have a genuine interest in protecting the girls.

It was a start.

With everything settled, Nicky got up to leave, and the guards came in to escort Fred back to his cell. As she made her way down the cold prison halls, Nicky felt like she was closer than ever to finding out the truth about Rosie. She was closer to justice.

But there was still so much work to do.

Just as she was leaving, her phone buzzed in her pocket, and Nicky took it out.

Chief Eric Franco.

Her stomach fell. That almost certainly meant there was work.

"Chief," Nicky said into the phone.

"Lyons," he said. "I need you to get down to HQ fast. We have information on one of the missing girls... and it's not pretty."

Nicky swallowed, hard. She didn't like the sound of that.

"I'll be right in."

CHAPTER TWO

Nicky walked into the Jacksonville FBI HQ and took the elevator, trying not to worry too much about what the chief had told her. She was putting her life on the line to help these girls, and she had to hope that she was doing the right thing--whatever he meant by "it's not pretty" hopefully didn't allude to the death of any of the victims on the top ten list of girls. At the request of Senator Amara Gregory, Nicky had been put in charge of a task force dedicated to finding ten missing girls across the country.

They'd found some alive.

Some, unfortunately, had died.

But Nicky had solved the crimes with the help of her partner, Ken Walker, and of course, the tech, Grace Taylor. They had a good team, and although Nicky had faced losses, she had to believe she could still save more girls.

The elevator dinged, and Nicky walked through the busy office to the briefing room. Inside, Ken and Grace were sitting at the table, and the chief was pacing across the front of the room by the overhead projector.

But he wasn't alone.

Senator Amara Gregory was there, too. Tall, slender, and dark-skinned, she was wearing a crisp orange dress and gave off an aura of authority. It had been a while since Nicky had last seen the woman who'd tasked her with this job—not since the first case, actually. Amara had been keeping tabs on the team, according to the chief, but she hadn't personally seen or reached out to Nicky in some time.

Nicky was still haunted by the memory of Maisie, the senator's daughter, who Nicky had been unable to save. Nicky's stomach twisted, because there had been so many other girls that she'd been unable to save too. She couldn't help but feel like a failure, like she'd been failing Senator Gregory all over again.

"Ah, Agent Lyons," the chief said. "Thank you for coming in on such short notice."

"What's going on?" Nicky asked, sitting across from Ken and Grace. She exchanged a glance with Ken, feeling his blue eyes bore into hers, and her chest warmed. Things had turned romantic between them--but Nicky was a professional. She wouldn't show emotion, not in front of the chief or the senator. But she was comforted by Ken's presence.

"You've all been doing a great job," Senator Gregory said. "I'm very sorry to hear that not every girl you've found so far could be recovered alive... but some of them have been, and at the very least, you've put killers behind bars."

A thick pause spread over the room. Nicky's gut twisted, and her fists balled. She felt like a failure. "I wish I had saved them all, Senator."

"Life doesn't always work out that way," the senator said. "I can tell by the reports that you three put your best feet forward… trust me when I say, I know it can't always work out…"

Nicky's gut twisted, thinking about Maisie, the poor girl who'd been kidnapped and killed, just moments before Nicky had arrived. If she'd been just a bit faster, then Senator Gregory would still have her daughter.

"They're fine agents," Franco said. "I wouldn't be surprised if they all made it to the SSA within a few years."

"That's the goal," Ken said. He smiled at Nicky, and she felt a little calmer.

"I'm glad to hear you say that," the senator said, looking at Franco. "I appreciate that, with everything going on in the world, you are keeping your priorities straight."

Franco nodded. "I try." He faced the agents, who were still sitting around the table.

The grim expression on his face made Nicky's heart drop.

"Unfortunately," the chief said, "we didn't call you all in to share good news. One of the missing girls on the list has been found... but she's not alive."

All at once, the room froze. Nicky's pulse pounded against her eardrums. *No--that can't be happening...*

Another girl was dead, and Nicky hadn't even had the chance to save her? How was she supposed to reconcile with that? She was still reeling with guilt over seeing Amara Gregory in person and thinking about Maisie—and now this, too?

She really needed a drink.

"She was found dead?" Ken asked when Nicky didn't, but Nicky was at a loss for words. Part of her didn't even want to know where this was going, unsure if her stomach could take it.

No—snap out of it, she told herself. She was an agent. She was trained for this. She *could* handle it.

"Yes," Franco said. "We're sorry to break the news so bluntly, but it's the truth." Franco was pacing the front of the room again, and Nicky heard the clack of his heels against the tile floor, but all she could think about was how it was too late. Too late for the girl who died. Too late for Nicky to save her.

She'd already lost too many.

Without another word, the chief tossed two print-outs on the table--photocopies of what looked to be Polaroid photos.

In one photo, a brown-haired girl was lying in a white dress with her throat slit. In the other, a girl slouched in a chair, also with her throat slit. The images made Nicky's gut churn with nausea—there was something old about them, something vintage, like they were pulled straight from the '70s.

Nicky looked closer at the first photo... she had seen this girl before…

It was her.

Paris Conner.

One of the girls from the list.

Nicky's mind raced, and anxiety tore through her. She couldn't lose it in front of the chief or the senator. She couldn't break down. But it was too much.

"It shocked us too," the chief said solemnly. "Like I said, you are a fine team of fine agents, but the reality is, we always knew not every girl could be recovered." He cleared his throat and glanced at Amara. "But we are starting to lose more than expected, and we really can't afford to lose any more."

Nicky's stomach bottomed out. She knew they were being professional about it, but it was clear: Nicky's task force was starting to fail.

She'd lost the most recent girl on the list.

And Paris Conner was gone before Nicky even got to look into her.

This was bad. Really bad. Forget Nicky's personal feelings, her own guilt and demons—this was bad for her team, for the FBI. It looked bad on her professionally, as an agent, and as the leader of this team.

"We want you to keep looking at the other girls on the list," Franco said, "but given the unique circumstances here, with Paris Conner's fate, we need you to do this first. We suspect more women are being taken by the sicko taking these photos."

"Where'd they come from?" Nicky asked.

"The one of Paris was found by a civilian in an antique store. The one of the other woman, who we're still working to identify, was found by police later in the same store."

Nicky looked closer at each photo. Paris was a brunette with pale skin and doe-like eyes.

The other girl... she fit the same description.

In fact, those girls looked so alike, they could be sisters.

"We're waiting on more details," the chief said, "but we're hoping to know more about the second victim soon."

"Do we have any idea where the bodies are?" Grace asked.

"Not at all," Franco said. "We're scouring the area and trying to get experts to see if they can track down where exactly these photos were taken, but... no hits yet. It looks like a basement of some kind."

"He could have more victims," Ken pointed out. "And the girls--they look a lot alike, don't they?"

"That's the danger here," Franco said. "This sicko could be preying on women who look very similar to each other... and we have to assume that he's going to take more."

Nicky chewed her lip as the men spoke. Her heart was racing, and she didn't know what to think. She was in charge of the team, and she felt like she was letting them down. She couldn't let them down... not now. She had to fight through these insecurities, now more than ever.

"We want you to find out what you can about these girls," Franco said. "Who they were, where they'd been last... anything you can get your hands on."

"We're all ears," Ken said.

"And we need you to keep this quiet," Amara said. "The media doesn't know about it yet. We don't want to give the killer any advantage."

Nicky nodded, taking it all in. "Understood."

"We'll keep you updated," said Franco, pointing at Nicky. "But Agent Lyons is the lead on this."

"Got it."

"I'm sorry it's so soon after the last girl," the chief said, "but this is a serious matter. I know the task force is having a hard time finding and saving these girls, but we need you to keep your eyes open. This killer--or killers--is getting bolder. We may have a serial killer on our hands."

Nicky felt the weight of the statement. As much as it discouraged her to know they'd already lost Paris Conner, she had to stay strong and continue being the head of this team. Not every mission had been a failure. But Nicky had to admit her self-confidence was taking a hit.

"You're dismissed," Chief Franco said. "Everything we currently know is in those files right there. Go over your game plan and head out."

With that, both the chief and Amara left the room. Nicky was left with Ken and Grace, who were all at a loss for words. Nicky chewed on her lip, feeling the weight of the pressure. Being a leader was never going to be an easy task—she knew that when she'd accepted the job, but sometimes… sometimes she just wished she had an "undo" button.

"Nicky?" Grace asked, and Nicky met her eyes. "You okay?"

Nicky forced a small smile. She could tell by the stern look on Ken's face that he was thinking the same thing as Grace—they could sense Nicky's doubts in herself, no matter how hard she tried to look strong, and that made her feel uncomfortably vulnerable, even in front of Ken.

"I'm good," she said. "Let's just focus on finding this bastard as quickly as possible so we can save the rest of the girls on the list. We can't..." She took a breath. "We can't lose any more."

"We'll get him," Ken said. He grabbed the file and opened it. "Looks like the shop is in a small town about an hour north called Pine Grove. Lyons, what's our plan?"

She took a breath, going over it in her mind. "Grace, you stay here and stand by until we need you. Walker, you and I will head out."

"Where are we going first?" Ken asked.

Nicky stood up, her eyes lingering on those eerie Polaroid photos. "Let's start with the antique store."

CHAPTER THREE

Nicky took a breath as she drove, the open highway in front of her as they made their way through Northern Florida to Pine Grove. Ken was in the passenger seat going over the files, but they'd been quiet for some time. The sun was swollen in the mid-morning sky, but Nicky was feeling anything but peaceful.

She just wanted to get this case solved. The more time she had to drive, the more time she had to think about Paris Conner, and how Nicky had failed to find her before it was too late.

She knew she couldn't do anything about the past, but it was still so hard to accept that Paris was gone. Nicky didn't know the girl on a personal level—of course not—but she remembered what it was like to be kidnapped. She remembered how it was to feel alone and unsure. How hard it was to just look ahead. She remembered how terrifying it was, being under the total control of a madman.

Nicky wanted to save these girls, and she wanted to get the sick bastards who were doing this to them. She hated the idea of letting evil win. Those girls—they had lives, and they deserved to live them, not have them ripped away because of some delusional madman's sick fantasies.

"You okay?" Ken asked.

Nicky looked over at him. "Yeah... just thinking."

"About what?"

"About the case," she said. "About the girls."

"I hear you," Ken said. "But don't let it get to you. We'll get the bastard who took Paris and the other girls. I can tell you're feeling…"

He trailed off. But Nicky prompted him to go on. Was she that transparent?

"Feeling what?"

"Doubtful," Ken clarified. "I don't know, maybe I'm imagining it, but I feel like your resolve is dying."

"It's not," Nicky lied. "Not at all."

She sighed. What was she lying for? This was Ken—her partner—the guy she was falling for. Nicky nodded, but she felt the weight of the case on her shoulders. She didn't want to feel like she was failing her team, but it was a possibility.

"I just don't want to let them down," she confessed. "I don't know what else I can do. It's like I'm always a few steps behind lately. We couldn't save Amanda Smith, or Clara Jones, and now--"

"Hey, don't think like that," Ken cut in. “We can’t save everybody, Lyons, and that’s one of the hardest things to reconcile with this job—but you know it; it’s what you signed up for too.”

Nicky felt his warm hand gently touch her thigh, and she sucked in a breath. She glanced at Ken, who had an intense look in his blue eyes. Her heart thrummed wildly, feeling the contact between their bodies, still so foreign to her.

Nicky and Ken had deepened their relationship recently--they'd confessed their feelings for each other, but neither of them had truly acted upon it. They'd hugged, but they hadn't kissed, or even come close. But Nicky felt safe with Ken. She felt like he'd protect her and take care of her, and she knew those were good things to want in a partner.

Nicky took a deep breath. She was starting to feel so overwhelmed. She hadn't truly realized how badly the case was affecting her, but now that she was thinking about it, she knew she had to get it together.

"You're not letting them down," Ken said. "We'll get the bastard who did this. I know it."

Nicky took a deep breath and nodded. She knew that Ken was just trying to make her feel better, but she needed to believe him.

"And the team is in good shape," he went on. "We have the files, and we have his killing pattern. We have everything we need to figure this out. Just like we did with the other girls. Just like we'll do with this case."

Nicky nodded. Somehow, Ken always managed to put her at ease. He made her feel like she was strong and capable, and he never let her doubt herself. It was refreshing, and it was something she needed right now.

She felt like they could be close without anything going wrong between them.

"Just think about this case," Ken said. "Let's find the bastard who took Paris and make him pay for what he did. We'll save the other girls too."

"I know... it's just..."

"You're doing your best, Nicky. Don't worry about the past. Don't worry about the future. Just focus on now."

She appreciated that she could be vulnerable with him. Nicky had always kept a strong head, even when she didn't feel it, but with Ken she could let those walls down, and let him help boost her up. She'd never had that before.

"You're right," Nicky said. "I'll try not to let it get to my head. Thanks for the pep talk."

They fell quiet, listening to the lull of the car on the road. Ken re-focused on the files. After a moment, he continued talking.

"Hey, maybe it's not the time, but..."

Nicky's heart picked up, and she glanced at him to see he was looking at his lap. For a moment, they felt a lot less like partners--and more like something else.

"I was thinking, after all this is over, we could spend some time together. You know, outside of work."

Nicky's face instantly flushed. "Are you asking me on a date, Walker?"

His cheeks were red. "I... yeah. I don't know how formal I'm supposed to be about it. I mean, I don't want to freak you out by asking you to marry me or something..."

Nicky laughed, and she felt her heart lighten. She never would have expected that Ken Walker, of all people, would be the first to ask her out. And she definitely never would have expected that she'd say yes.

"I'd love to," she said. "I mean, after we get all this craziness behind us. I want to be sure that we're completely focused on our work."

"I know," Ken said. "And honestly, I don't want to rush into anything. I just... I feel like I've been waiting for this for a long time. I guess I've known for a while that I wanted to ask you out."

Nicky leaned over and kissed his cheek. She knew it was risky to do it, but she was so glad that she did. She didn't feel nervous at all, and she wasn't second-guessing herself. She was sure and calm. "I'm glad you did."

"Me too," Ken said. "I'm glad you said yes."

Before things could get mushy, Nicky said, "Let's focus on the case until then, though. Agreed?"

"Definitely," Ken said. "I just had to ask you while I had the balls to do it."

Nicky laughed, feeling light inside. At least one thing in her life seemed to be going in the right direction.

They went quiet for a while, and Ken flipped through the files on his lap. "You know," Ken said, "I'm reading the history of the town, and for being such a small place, Pine Grove sure has a lot of antique stores."

"That's a bit weird," Nicky agreed.

"It's like a tourist destination for thrifters," Ken continued. "They have old car festivals here too, some years. Really high population of seniors."

Nicky nodded. That could be relevant.

"Officers are already checking the other stores for more photos," Ken went on. "So hopefully they'll let us know ASAP if they find any."

"Good," Nicky said. "The sick bastard who planted those photos might be storing others elsewhere."

"What kind of person would do that?" Ken asked. "Just take photos of women he's murdered and plant them in places for people to find? Hell, a kid could come across one of them and be traumatized for life."

"A twisted individual," Nicky said. As she drove, she dove into her years of knowledge on human psychology and behavioral analysis. If she had to guess, they were dealing with a killer who thought of himself as an "artist" of some kind. He got off on the thrill of putting these photos up, and he got off on the rush of doing something so sick, it would never be uncovered.

A chill ran up her spine as she pictured this man. He was out there somewhere… real… and she would find him.

"He's a sick bastard, that's for sure," Ken said.

"It's not really about the antique store, though," Nicky said, her eyes still on the road. "He's probably putting them up in a place where he thinks someone will find them. He's not just doing it for that thrill. He wants this to be exposed, in a way."

Serial killers often wanted to be the focus of attention, and the fact that this killer would choose to have his victims photographed and put on display was a big clue that he wanted people to know what he'd done.

"How sick," Nicky said. "He wants to show off his accomplishments, as if he's won some sick game. It's like he's trying to be famous for killing."

Ken nodded. "It's like taking pride in it."

"He's proud of what he's done," Nicky said. "And he wants people to know it."

A psychopath. Someone who was completely devoid of any empathy. She knew that the FBI had a lot of resources at its disposal, but they still didn't have a lot of information on the guy. To find him, they'd have to get a whole lot more. Until then, all Nicky could do was speculate on who he might be, creating phantom images of him in her mind.

But he was real, and he was out there, lurking, maybe even looking for his next victim. She clenched her teeth tight. No—letting that happen was not an option.

They drove on for a long time, until the sun was high in the sky. Nicky knew that there weren't many towns in the world where one might find an antique shop on every street corner. She wondered if that was just because Pine Grove was so small, or if there was something else to it. Something she hadn't really considered.

She wasn't sure what she was about to find out. But she was ready for it.

There were people out there relying on her to save their lives.

CHAPTER FOUR

Nicky sped the car past Pine Grove's population sign. They had driven through a light marshland to get here, and it was in the middle of nowhere, Northern Florida. As the car slowed to a safe speed limit, Nicky took note of the small houses that emerged around them. Up ahead, she could see the downtown strip, equipped with a church and clock tower.

"Do you think it's possible that the killer is from here?" Ken asked. "Maybe he's someone who's lived here all his life."

"Maybe," Nicky said. "But it's also likely that he picked this place because it was isolated, and he had a good chance of planting the photos without being seen."

"Good point," Ken said.

"So, we're looking for a guy who's had access to a Polaroid camera. And he's either in Pine Grove or very familiar with it." Nicky rubbed her chin as she drove. "I don't know how much help that'll be, but it's a start."

"It's more than we had before we got here," Ken said. "Hopefully we'll find more answers at the antique shop."

"The police should still be there." Nicky pressed harder on the gas, tempted to speed, but kept herself at a steady pace. They were almost there.

Ken's phone began to buzz, and he quickly answered it. "This is Agent Walker." He put it on speaker so Nicky could hear.

"This is Chief Gammage of the Pine Grove PD," he said. "I was informed to call you in case we came up with any more hits on photographs found at other antique stores in town."

Nicky's chest tightened, and Ken had an intense look on his face.

"And?" Ken pressed.

"Nothing yet," Gammage said through the phone.

"Chief Gammage, this is Agent Lyons," Nicky cut in. "Please keep your personnel looking. I need you to call in troopers and get them to branch the search out to other towns too. There could be way more of those photographs out there."

"Roger that, agents," he said.

The call ended, and Ken tucked his phone away. Nicky bit her lip. She really hoped that the killer wasn't planting these photos all over the country, or else this might take a lot longer.

"What are you thinking?" Ken asked.

"Just worried about how far this has stretched out," Nicky said. "We've only found two photos here, at the same store in Pine Grove, so let's hope he's sticking to this area."

"True, or we'd have a lot of other towns to search," Ken said. "And that doesn't even take into account the fact that the killer could be planting these photos in other states. If he's staying in a small town, then he has a much smaller victim pool."

"I suppose you're right," Nicky said. "But at least we won't have to search the entire continental U.S. Paris Conner was from Miami, right?"

Ken went into the files, flipping through pages. "That's right. Her parents are realtors and own a hell of a lot of property over there."

Nicky bit into her lip. "So how did a photo of her body end up in Northern Florida, at some antique shop in a small town?"

"I hope we find out, Lyons."

As soon as they pulled into the parking lot of the antique shop, they could see the car that belonged to the police officer who'd been stationed outside. He was probably inside, talking with the owner. The sign of the store was an old, weathered, wooden board, with the words HARRIET ANTIQUES painted in large, bold letters. The paint had faded over time, but the letters could still be discerned, each one carefully painted to achieve a vintage look. Surrounding the sign were rows of rusting iron signposts that used to hold old street signs, and behind it was the antique shop itself, a small brick building with numerous windows and quaint awnings.

Ken and Nicky got out of the car and walked toward the store, not wasting any time to go inside. The bell on the door dinged, and Nicky was instantly met with the musty, woody smell of the antique shop. There was fading damask wallpaper, blue and yellow, on the walls. There were many things inside, ranging from paintings to vases to china to a sofa.

The owner was an elderly man with pale skin and a thick head of white hair. He didn't look like he'd ever stopping smiling a day in his life. Across the counter from him was a young officer in a standard blue uniform.

"Officer, thank you for your assistance," Nicky said, holding up her badge. "I'm Agent Lyons FBI."

The officer shook her hand and nodded at Ken. "Of course. I'm Officer Jim. This is the owner of the shop, Mr. Dumond."

"Delighted to meet you," Mr. Dumond said. "I'm not used to so much... anxiety in the store."

"I'm sorry for this, sir," Nicky said. "We're hoping you can give us more information on what happened."

"Of course," Mr. Dumond said. "I'm happy to help in any way I can. I've been living in Pine Grove since I was a little boy. To think something awful happened to one of the young women here is just terrible."

Officer Jim stepped out, leaving Nicky and Ken to talk to Mr. Dumond alone.

"Actually," Nicky said, "we can confirm the identity of one of the victims, and she was not a Pine Grove resident." She paused to take a deep breath. "It's possible that the killer took the photo elsewhere, then came to town to plant it here."

Mr. Dumond's eyes grew wide. "So, do you think it was one of my customers?" he asked.

"At this point it's still too early to tell," Nicky said. "But I do want to go through some of your photographs to see if we can find any more."

"Of course," Mr. Dumond said. He stepped behind the counter and took out a small box. "The police already went through most of them, but I kept the photos here, just in case the police wanted to look at them again."

As Mr. Dumond handed her the box, Nicky was struck by the man's eyes. They were so full of life and happiness. She found it hard to believe that he could be responsible for anything that had happened here. If he was, he was certainly a very convincing actor.

As she looked through the photos, Nicky couldn't help but get distracted by all the old photographs. Most of them were vintage, and didn't seem to be taken with the same camera as the photos of the victims. The photos of the victims were a more tall, thin style of Polaroid.

"Most of these photos have been here for years," Mr. Dumond said. "They're not necessarily for sale. I mean, if someone wanted them, they could buy them, but I mostly keep them out near the vintage cameras to give the area some life." He wrung his hands together. "I have no idea who put those other photos in, or when."

"Do you have any other employees?" Nicky asked.

"No," Mr. Dumond said.

Nicky exchanged a look with Ken, then nodded.

"We can safely assume somebody casually came in and dropped them," Nicky said. "Can you think of anyone strange or suspicious who you've seen in the shop in recent months?"

"Goodness, no," he said. "My customers are mostly locals, and they're all so sweet. We have a high elderly population here, you see, which is why so many of us antique enthusiasts settle down here. We draw in crowds of antique lovers from all over the country."

"I guess there are a lot of antique enthusiasts in Pine Grove," Ken said.

"Oh, yes," Mr. Dumond said. "Most of the people in this town are really into the old ways. I mean, we still have a town square where people just hang out and talk. It's so quaint!"

"Sounds like a nice place to live," Ken said.

"Oh, it is!" Mr. Dumond said. "It's got a nice, small town feel to it. I live a good distance outside of town, but I come in most days for work. I'm lucky enough to have my own shop, and don't need to worry about a boss."

"I suppose that's true," Nicky said. "And I'm sure you've seen just about everybody in town."

"Just about," Mr. Dumond confirmed. "I know most of my regulars, and I remember all their faces. I'm sorry, I don't mean to be rude, but I do get a little excited about antique shop talk."

"But you also said you get a lot of tourists, so you must be used to new faces too," Nicky pointed out. "So, if a stranger came in, it wouldn't be odd."

"Yes, that's correct. We get many tourists as well."

"Right," Nicky said. "One more question, Mr. Dumond. Do you have security footage?"

A Cheshire cat-like smile took over his face. "As a matter of fact, I do."

CHAPTER FIVE

Nicky felt a wave of relief wash over her as she stood in the antique shop. The security footage could help them find more answers, no doubt.

"Can we take a look at it?" Nicky asked.

"Without a doubt," Mr. Dumond said. "You know, I forgot to mention it to the police, although they didn't ask to see it."

"That's what we're here for," Ken said.

Mr. Dumond led them behind the counter, to a small room, an area where he had a desk, a cabinet, and a desktop computer. He sat at the desk and opened the computer. "I just need to bring up the system."

The computer was built in the style of a decade ago, with a bulky tower and a large screen. The screen flickered on, revealing a login request.

"Is this the same computer you've always had here?" Nicky asked.

"Yes. It doesn't do me much good," Mr. Dumond said. "We don't have a theft issue in this town." He looked up at them and wagged his finger. "I can't believe that I forgot to tell the police about this. I'm so sorry."

"Don't worry about it," Nicky said. "We're just glad you remembered."

"I have a terrible memory," Mr. Dumond said. "But it's not so bad when it comes to my work. I mean, I don't forget what a gramophone is, or a sandwich-board. But I can't remember if I put my keys in my left pocket or my right."

He indicated for them to sit down at his desk, and Nicky and Ken obliged.

"We need to see footage from the last month, at least," Nicky said. "We can assume someone else would have noticed the photos if they'd been here for too long."

"That's true," Mr. Dumond said. "I've had kids in here looking through them, and no one ever brought those awful pictures to my attention, so I'm not sure how long they were here."

"And the woman who found them," Ken said, "she didn't bring the photo to you?"

"Oh, no," Mr. Dumond said. "She left right away, understandably so, and then all of a sudden the police were at my door!"

"Right," Nicky said. She'd been informed that the witness was a customer named June who had brought the photos down to the station. The police had first questioned Mr. Dumond but he wasn't, at present, a person of interest. Nicky didn't suspect him either; she'd seen wolves in sheep's skin before, but Mr. Dumond seemed genuinely nice. Of course, nothing could be ruled out.

Until then, though, Nicky needed to see that security footage.

"Let's start, then," Nicky said.

He tapped on the keyboard, and the footage began to show. "I'm afraid I have mostly normal customers, but I keep it on a loop so I can catch anyone who comes in after I close."

The footage started off with a bright flash of light, and then the view was suddenly of Mr. Dumond opening the shop. "This is the footage from yesterday."

The three of them watched as Mr. Dumond opened the shop and began his day. He was a simple man, and the footage didn't show anything out of the ordinary.

After a few minutes, Mr. Dumond turned to them. "You can fast-forward through a lot of this," he said. "You're probably better with this technology than I am."

Nicky took up his invitation and scooted closer to the computer, using the keyboard to fast-forward through footage.

They saw customers coming in and out of the store. Mostly elderly people, the odd family with kids. No one suspicious. They skimmed through the entirety of the last week and found nothing. Whoever dropped the photos into the shop was lucky to have gotten them in without being caught. She didn't need to look at the footage to know that whoever it was had committed a crime, but the footage could prove it.

They had to keep looking.

Nicky sped into two weeks ago, watching as people came and went from the store. Again, mostly elderly, sometimes families, or generally normal seeming people. Some went to the camera area at the back, some didn't. This was beginning to feel like a wild goose chase, until--

A man in a black hoodie entered the store, his face concealed from the camera. He looked around, but they couldn't make out his ethnicity or anything. Looking over his shoulder, the man then darted to the back of the store and did what looked like rummaging with the camera area.

All the while, Mr. Dumond was busy talking to a customer at the counter.

Bingo.

"Do you remember this man?" Nicky asked.

"Oh, not at all," Mr. Dumond said. "He must have slipped right past me."

"Did he take anything?" Ken asked.

"I don't think so," Mr. Dumond said. "I didn't notice anyone taking anything."

Nicky's heart raced. This man--this blurry, faceless man--could be their guy. In fact, she was almost certain of it.

But the only thing they could make out about him was that he was male, of moderate build, and could be anywhere from twenty-five to in his forties, judging by the way he walked.

"Do you have any cameras on the parking lot?" Nicky asked.

"I do," Mr. Dumond said. "All these security systems were left from the previous owners; I've never had the need for them."

"Can we see that footage?" Ken asked.

Again, Mr. Dumond clicked the mouse, and a different set of footage began to play. This one showed the parking lot.

And there was the man, leaving the store, heading to a car. But the footage only showed part of the parking lot. They saw the man go up to a vehicle, but they could only make out the bottom half of its frame--no logo or license plate.

"Damn," Nicky said.

"You're a car girl," Ken said, "I don't suppose you can identify that by looking at the bottom of it?"

Nicky squinted to see clearer. She could tell by the shape and aesthetic that it was an older car, likely from the ‘90s.

"It's a sedan," she said. "An older model, probably from the ‘90s, I think. Maybe a Japanese brand. It's dark in color. Looks like its dark green, maybe forest green, but that's all I can get from this..."

Nicky knew cars, and she knew them well. There was something distinctly Japanese in style about the shape of this car, but it didn't look like a mainstream brand. It could have been one of the many competitors in the ‘90s, who ended up being bought out by larger corporations and forgotten by history.

Nicky took out her phone. She could feel it--some sort of memory associated with a car frame of that style. She looked up Japanese car brands from the ‘90s and scrolled through the list, scanning the various models and shapes of vehicles. Her eyes were trained and her fingers moved over the phone screen with deft precision, searching for some hint or clue that might help her identify the car in the parking lot. She scrutinized each entry carefully, trying to pinpoint any key similarities that could help her narrow down the possibilities. As she scrolled through the list, her expression grew more and more focused, her mind racing with possibilities as she tried to pinpoint the elusive vehicle.

"What are you doing, Lyons?"

"I think I know what it is," Nicky said. "Just give me a second."

"Wow, very impressive," said Mr. Dumond.

And there, Nicky spotted it.

Hana. A brand that once existed in the '90s but ended up going out of business. Nicky held up a picture of a Hana sedan to the security footage.

"Looks like a match," Ken said.

"That's not all," Nicky said. "This is a Hana Kuma."

"Really?" Ken said. "I've never heard of it."

"It's a sedan that was originally designed in Japan, but for a while they had a production facility here in America. But they went bankrupt years ago. In fact, you can't buy them anymore, only restore them."

"Are you sure?" Ken asked. "Because it doesn't look like anything special to me."

"My dad used to have one," Nicky said. "He restored it when I was a kid."

The memory struck her like a chord. That was why she recognized it. Her dad had one. Nicky had learned most of what she knew about cars from her father. As much of a deadbeat as he was, she knew that letting her watch while he worked on cars was one of the few good things he did for her development.

And he'd loved that Hana. When it broke down, he'd spend weeks restoring it. He'd even added a custom touch to it, something that Nicky never figured out.

"Well, I'll be damned," Ken said. "Then we know who our mystery man is."

"We know that the photos were dropped off by a Hana Kuma," Nicky said. "We don't know who was driving it."

"But we can find out," Ken said.

Nicky stood up, feeling determined. "Right. We need to get some traffic footage from the local police."

That would take time, and they didn't have much. If the man from the Hana Kuma turned out to be the same man from the photos, he could escape any day now.

They didn't have any time to waste.

CHAPTER SIX

The light in the basement flickered on, and the man smiled gleefully at his latest prize.

Sitting in a chair, underneath the light, was a beautiful brunette woman. The woman sat with her head bowed in fear as the man loomed over her. She was dressed in a simple but elegant black dress, her dark hair cascading down her slender neck. Her features were delicate and finely wrought, with full lips and smoldering brown eyes.

She was perfect. The perfect subject for his photoshoot.

"Aren't you so pretty, doll?" he asked her. "You've been told that your whole life, haven't you? So pretty. Such a pretty girl."

"P-please," she managed, "please let me go. I'll do whatever you want, just let me go."

"Ah, there's the problem, doll. See, you're not in control anymore. I am. I'm the master, and you are the pet."

"No, no, I-"

"Look at me."

She looked up, her beautiful eyes meeting his.

"You're a pretty girl, aren't you? So pretty."

"Please," she sobbed, tears running down her face, "let me go. I promise I won't tell anyone. Just let me go."

"Oh, I won't let you go," he told her sweetly. "I'm going to keep you here."

"Please," she begged, "don't hurt me."

"Oh, I'm not going to hurt you, doll. I just want to take some pictures. You won't even notice the pain."

"No," she begged again, "no, I won't let you take pictures of me."

"Oh, we'll see about that," he grinned, and raised his camera.

"You see, doll," he explained, "you're such a pretty girl, and you're going to be so beautiful in the pictures I take. You're the subject of my photography. Aren't you happy? You should be."

"No, please--I just want to go home, please..."

But he wouldn't let her go home. Not yet. Not ever. In fact, he was going to dress her up like a model. Smiling, he went over to the locker and pulled it open to reveal many dresses for her to choose from.

"Ah, so many pretty dresses for my pretty doll," he laughed. He pulled the door open and gestured for the woman to come forward. Obediently she stood and walked toward the open locker. Slowly, one by one, he held up each dress and waited for her to shake her head no, then threw it back into the locker. She was crying now, as he threw dress after dress back into the locker. Then he smiled wider and held up a small pink one. She nodded meekly and he pulled it out.

"Oh, this one is perfect!" he exclaimed, holding it up to her.

"Y-yes," she stammered, "it's lovely."

"Let me help you," he said, and pulled a pair of scissors from his pocket.

"What--what are you going to do?" she whimpered.

"Oh, I'm just going to make some alterations to this dress," he said, and cut a hole in the front of her dress. He pulled a knife from his pocket and cut off the sleeves. He pulled the dress over her head, then cut off the skirt.

"Oh, my--you're lovely," he cooed.

He loved the way it looked on her, and he knew she'd look even more beautiful in it than the other models.

"There we go," he told her. "Now, you look like a girl."

"Please," she begged, "just let me go. I don't want to be here anymore."

"Oh, you'll be here for a long time, pretty girl," he told her, gently stroking her face.

"Please, don't touch me," she begged.

"Oh, but I have to touch you. I have to touch you all over. I have to touch you where I want to. I have to touch your pretty, pretty face."

He ran his hand across her cheek, and she backed away, as far as she could go.

"Please, don't hurt me," she pleaded.

"Oh, doll, you're the most perfect subject for a photoshoot. You're so pretty, and you're so scared. I love it. I love you."

"Please, don't hurt me."

"Oh, little one," he said, "I'm not going to hurt you. I'm here to make you beautiful."

They never appreciated the work he was doing, not enough. They didn't realize that they were part of the greatest photography exhibit the world would ever see. And it was all made by him.

He would be famous. He would earn what he had always deserved and show the world what they were missing out on by not appreciating his artistic talent.

All of those fools... he would show them all what he was worth.

This model was too beautiful to pass up. He would like to see them find someone so young and beautiful. His perfect doll.

"You're mine now," he said. "All I have to do is prepare you... tell me... do you prefer pink or red lipstick?"

He moved toward her, then, and she backed away. She knew that there was no escaping, and perhaps she would be better off if she accepted the inevitable.

"Please," she begged, "please just let me go. I won't tell anyone. Just let me go."

"Oh, doll, I'm not going to let you go," he said, and picked up his camera. "I'm not going to let you go ever. I'm going to make sure you're my little doll forever."

"No, please, I know you're taking pictures of me but--"

"But nothing," he told her, and put his camera to his face. "Smile, doll."

She tried to smile, and he clicked the camera. She was so beautiful, so innocent.

"That's good, doll," he told her. "You're a good model."

"No, no, no," she cried, "please, don't do this... please..."

He was going to take so many pictures of her. So many pictures. He'd take her to the top of the world.

The man clicked the camera again and again and again. He wanted to capture all of the beauty in one frame.

This one was going to be his masterpiece.

CHAPTER SEVEN

Nicky pushed through the doors at the Pine Grove precinct with Ken behind her. They didn't have a second to waste--Nicky was certain that the car on the security footage was a Hana Kuma sedan, and if it was, then chances were that it was the only one in town. But she needed to see more of the car, to see its exact year and model, and the officers here would surely have access to all the traffic cameras around town.

You could tell a lot about a person from their car. The type of car they drove, the condition it was in, and how they treated it, all helped to form a profile of the driver.

They walked up to the young deputy behind the desk and held up their badges. He looked up at them, shocked.

"Wow, I heard the FBI was here, but--"

"We need to access the traffic cameras," Nicky cut in. "We're looking to identify the driver of a specific car, who should have been driving through town on August 18th."

"I can definitely get that for you," the officer said. "Come on, I'll bring you to the security room."

The deputy led them down a hallway, past a few closed doors. Nicky tried to peer through the windows in the doors, but she couldn't make out anything. They walked through another door and stepped into a small room that contained three desks, each with a computer.

The deputy pointed to one of the desks. "All the footage is uploaded here. It's organized by day, and time of day. You can watch the video right there. Here are the login details."

"Thank you," Nicky said.

They sat down at the desk and the deputy left the room. Nicky turned on the computer, opened the folder, and pulled up the video.

There were a small handful of traffic cameras throughout the town, mostly at major intersections. There was a red light near Harriet Antiques, so that's what they were looking for. Nicky already knew the exact date and time to look for the car and see it at a stoplight, so she skimmed through the footage until she found the right timestamp.

The footage showed the stoplight at the intersection of Maple and Oak, and the vehicle in question could be seen in the top right corner of the screen, waiting to make a right turn. It was a dark blue sedan. Nicky leaned in, watching intently, craning her neck to get a better view of the license plate.

But there was no license plate at all.

Nicky squinted, but she was definitely seeing it right. No license plate.

And the car was in rough shape. It was rusting and looked like it hadn't been tended to in years, which was nothing like the car Nicky's father had restored all those years ago. In many ways, her father had cared more for that car than he had Nicky.

But this one was clearly in rough shape, which told her a few things about the owner:

To him, the car was a junker. Not worth taking care of. Either that, or he was a low-income individual and didn't have the money for the upkeep. But other things felt more deliberate:

It had no license plate, which meant he knew he didn't want to get tracked.

It had a cracked windshield, which meant it was even harder to identify him.

In fact, even when Nicky zoomed in--there was no clear picture of the driver at all.

"We'll have to go through more cameras in the town and see if we can get an ID on his face," Nicky said. "The good news is, we can identify the model. That's a 1998. It's one of the last ones they ever made."

"So, we have a car make, a year, and a location," Ken said. "That's a start."

She turned back to the computer. "We should start checking other intersections around town."

"That's going to take a while," Ken said. "How many intersections are there in town?"

"I don't know," Nicky said. "Enough that this is going to eat at our time."

Just then, Nicky's phone rang in her pocket. She pulled it out--Chief Franco. Her heart dropped.

"Hold on, Walker," she told Ken. "It's the chief. You keep looking through security footage."

"On it."

Nicky stepped away and answered the phone. "This is Agent Lyons."

"Lyons," the chief said, "I wanted to call you myself and let you know we've got an ID on the second victim."

Nicky swallowed, hard. "And?"

"Her name is Francine Gibbons. Like Paris Conner, her parents are powerful people with great standing—and a lot of money. I'm sending you over her file. Review it carefully."

With that, the call ended. Nicky sighed and faced Ken.

"What's up?" he asked. "What did the chief say?"

"They identified the second victim," she said.

"And?"

"It was Francine Gibbons. The chief is emailing me her file." Nicky pulled out her laptop and set it up on the table.

She skimmed the file, and she could see why the chief had called her personally. Francine Gibbons, who went by Frankie, had a very privileged upbringing. She was the child of a Senator and a wealthy socialite, with two older brothers and a sister. She'd grown up in a large, secluded, and gated mansion in the hills, and was a regular on the town's social scene from a young age. She'd grown up in a small, wealthy community not far from Jacksonville.

Nicky scrolled through the file, reading about all the important events in her life:

She had graduated from the Rosewood private school, and then gone on to study at the prestigious Harvard University, where she'd majored in English. She'd been quite the bookworm--but she'd also been quite the party girl. She drank and smoked, but she'd never been in any serious trouble. She'd had a handful of scandals, but nothing that got her in deep.

That was, until, she'd been reported missing about two months ago.

Nicky paused. She grabbed her bag and pulled out Paris Conner's file.

Paris had been missing for eight months--that was why she'd ended up on the top ten list. And Francine, she had been missing for two months before the photo turned up.

Why was his timeline so stretched out?

When were the photos taken--and why did the killer wait so long to plant them?

All these questions racked Nicky's mind. She went back to Paris's file. Other than their similar appearance, and the fact that they both came from wealthy families, the girls didn't have much in common.

"I've seen the car in a few different spots," Ken said, "but we can't make out his face in any of the footage. He's a ghost."

"Damn," Nicky said. No luck there. But not all hope was lost. "We have two victims now," she said, "so maybe there's a connection. Maybe one of them knew who had a Hana Kuma sedan."

"Sounds like a job for Grace," Ken said.

He was absolutely right. Nicky took out her phone and called Grace. A young, but experienced tech, Nicky could always rely on Grace Taylor to find out hidden information fast.

"Agent Lyons," Grace said.

"It's me, Gracc," Nicky said. "Got a job for you."

"Sure thing, boss. What can I do for you?"

"I'm looking for a 1998 Hana Kuma that's in bad shape. It might belong to the killer. Can you see if anyone has one in their name with any connection to either Paris Conner or Francine Gibbons?"

"Oh, I'm on it, boss," Grace said. On the other end, Nicky could hear keys clacking. Ken sat across from Nicky, watching with interest, as they both waited for Grace to work her magic.

After a few moments--she did.

"You're not gonna believe this," Grace said. "Francine Gibbons's ex-boyfriend, Jimmy Drake, has that exact car registered to his name."

Nicky's mouth went dry. This could be him.

"Tell me everything about him."

"Well, he's not exactly a squeak- clean guy," Grace said. "Twenty-eight years old, long list of petty crimes under his belt, most of them petty theft, a few credit card frauds, and he's been under investigation for a while now for something a bit more serious."

"What's that?"

"Jimmy was suspected of dealing drugs, but the police never had concrete evidence against him," Grace said. "His family was never very well off, and he lives alone now."

"So, what's the story with him and Francine?" Nicky asked. "How does a girl like her end up with a guy like him?"

"Well, from what I can see, she was pretty serious about him," Grace said. "She broke up with him about a month before she was reported missing, but she was really torn up about it. She was really in love with him. I can tell by the things she posted about him--and their breakup--on social media."

"So, she was the one to break it off," Nicky noted. "Interesting."

What would make a guy like that suddenly turn, and decide to kill his ex-girlfriend--and a random girl who looked like her, months prior?

Nicky's stomach sank. "Can you check and see if he has any ties to Paris Conner?"

"On it," Grace said.

Nicky chewed on her lip as she waited for Grace to come back. The anticipation was killing her. They felt close--really close--but they needed just a bit more.

Moments later, Grace was back on the line. "I'm not seeing anything. But Jimmy lives twenty minutes from Francine's community, in another small town, pretty close to Pine Grove. I don't have any proof he was ever in Miami, not yet."

Miami, of course, was where Paris had been from--and where she'd gone missing. It was a long way from here, but it was entirely possible the killer had been there on business and happened upon Paris, or even was just visiting. Maybe he even went there to choose a wealthy Miami girl, for whatever sick reason. Either way, the car was more than enough to look into him.

"Thanks, Grace," Nicky said.

"Anytime, boss," Grace said. "I'm sending his address. Good luck."

Once off the phone with Grace, Nicky faced Ken. "Okay, we have some updates," Nicky said, as she and Ken went over the case. "Jimmy Drake, Francine Gibbons's ex, has that car registered under his name. And Grace hasn't found any direct ties to Paris, yet, but he's definitely worth investigating further."

"By the sounds of it, yeah," Ken said, standing up. "I'm done with all this sitting around. This bastard is going down today."

"I'll drive," Nicky said, standing up. She and Ken had been partners for a long time now, and they both knew what the other wanted without having to say anything. Nicky could tell from his tone of voice that he was ready to fight, and she was ready to fight with him.

CHAPTER EIGHT

The road stretched before Nicky, topped by a clear summer sky. They were taking the backroads, as Jimmy Drake's town--Stoneycreek--was only an hour away from Pine Grove. Nicky could feel the surge of the car beneath her, and it was exhilarating to belt down the backroads with so few cars around.

Ken sat in the passenger seat, and he'd been quiet on the drive up. Nicky wondered if he was thinking about their conversation earlier--about finally going on a date and getting things moving between them that way. She knew it hadn't been easy for him to ask, but she was grateful he had.

Nicky had a lot of commitment issues in previous relationships, but whatever she had with Ken--it felt real, for the first time in her life.

But as she was thinking it, driving silently along the road, she couldn't help but feel guilty.

Rosie never got to experience first love, or a first kiss, or anything like that.

She'd been only fifteen when the kidnapper got away with her. So many years had passed since then, and Nicky knew, statistically, it was unlikely her sister was still alive. Maybe it was crazy, but Nicky still felt connected to Rosie, like even through time and distance, their blood bond thrived.

Nicky just *felt* like Rosie was still alive out there.

She felt like Rosie was still out there, and she'd come back someday. Maybe not today, or even tomorrow, but one day, and then Nicky would have to answer for what she'd done.

At least, that was how Nicky usually felt. She had to admit, this case was getting to her a bit. After all, Paris Conner had been found already dead, and Paris's family had hoped she would come home too.

Nicky wondered if it was her hubris as an FBI agent that led her to believe she could bring Rosie back alive. Maybe this was all in her head, and everything with Felix and the supposed 'mentor' was all for nothing.

"I've been thinking about something," Ken said, breaking the silence. "I want you to know that if you aren't ready, I'm not going to be upset."

Nicky turned her head to look at him, but she didn't answer. She wondered what she'd done to trigger him into thinking she'd changed her mind.

"What I said earlier," Ken said, "I meant it. I really like you, and I really want to take you out on a date. It's just that I don't want you to feel like I'm pressuring you, or trying to make you feel like you have to do anything you're not ready for."

"Thanks, Ken," Nicky said. "I appreciate that. I really do. But where's this coming from? I already said yes."

"I don't know." Ken awkwardly laughed. "I'm just so bad at this. I know I'm thirty-five, but my experience with women is, well..."

Nicky's heart sank as she remembered Ken's past. He'd dated a girl in high school, who had ended up being murdered. It was a huge motivator for Ken to join the FBI.

"I'm bad at it too," Nicky said. "We're both figuring this out, but... I want to try."

"Yeah?" Ken asked.

"Yeah," Nicky said, smiling. "I'm ready."

He returned her smile. "I mean it, Nicky. I'm not going to make you do anything you don't want to. This is just me telling you that I like you, and if you're ready, I'm ready. If you aren't, I'll wait for you."

Nicky gripped the steering wheel tight, her knuckles turning white. If she was ready? Was she ready? She didn't know. She'd never been in a real relationship before, and she had to admit, part of her was afraid of what it might mean for her career. If Nicky dated Ken, and it didn't work out, then what would happen to their partnership?

No--she couldn't think like that.

"Stop trying to make me doubt myself, Walker," Nicky said teasingly.

Ken laughed. "Sorry, I'll stop. I'm glad you said yes."

When Ken put his hand on her thigh, Nicky's heart skipped a beat. His hand felt so warm, and she didn't want him to move it.

Nicky nodded, and they drove in silence, until they reached the small town of Stoneycreek.

***

Nicky parked across the street from Jimmy's house and waited in the car with Ken for a moment, scouting the place. Jimmy Drake lived in a small house on the outskirts of Stoneycreek. It was a quiet neighborhood, lower class, nothing like where Francine had lived. The house was set back from the road, surrounded by overgrown grass and a neglected garden. It seemed unkempt and worn, a far cry from the elegant homes in Francine's neighborhood. The neighborhood itself was quiet, with empty streets and shuttered windows.

"Sure this is the right place?" Ken asked.

"It's what Grace found," Nicky said, turning off the car, and they got out.

Nicky and Ken walked up to the front door of Jimmy's house, and knocked. No one answered. Nicky stepped back and took a good look. It was a one-story house, with a front porch, and a small yard. The roof was gray, with dark shingles. The paint was peeling, the porch boards were cracked, and the windows were foggy.

"Maybe no one's home," Ken said.

"No..." Nicky muttered. "He's here."

She banged harder on the door.

"Jimmy Drake!" Nicky yelled. "Open up. We need to talk to you!"

She banged on the door, again and again. Nicky heard a movement inside the house, and she froze. The door opened, and Jimmy stood there, looking at them. His legs were bare, and he was wearing a dirty wife-beater, with no pants. His eyes were bloodshot, and he smelled of booze.

"What? Who are you?" he asked.

Nicky and Ken held up their badges.

"Agent Nicky Lyons, FBI," she said. "This is my partner, Agent Ken Walker. We need to talk to you about Francine Gibbons."

Jimmy's eyes widened. "Frankie? What about her?"

She exchanged a look with Ken. Frankie had just been ID'd, so there was a good chance the news of her discovery genuinely hadn't reached Jimmy yet. But Nicky had a pretty good idea that Jimmy already knew Frankie was dead.

Maybe he'd even killed her.

But she couldn't get ahead of herself. They needed more information first.

"May we come in?" Nicky asked.

Jimmy stepped aside. "Yeah, yeah. Whatever."

Nicky walked into the living room, and she was immediately greeted by the smell of booze and cigarettes. The living room was messy, with empty beer bottles on tables and overflowing ashtrays on the floor, as well as discarded clothes and trash.

Jimmy closed the door, and dropped down on the couch, putting his feet up.

Nicky glanced at Ken, and saw he was holding back disgust. She knew that Ken had a thing about people who didn't keep their houses clean, and she had to admit: he had a point.

Jimmy looked between Nicky and Ken. "So, what's this about Frankie?"

"Francine Gibbons has been identified as one of two homicide victims," Nicky said, saying it blankly to gauge Jimmy's reaction.

It seemed to wake him up. His eyes went wide. "Wait, sorry, what? You're telling me Frankie is, what, dead or something?"

Nicky and Ken were quiet.

"You seem surprised," Nicky commented. "You know Francine has been missing for two months."

"Well yeah, but I figured she ran away after I dumped her," Jimmy said. "She was really torn up about the whole thing."

"Why would you 'dump' her?" Ken asked. "She was a nice girl, was she not? A rich girl, a girl with a wealthy family..."

"Yeah--but come on, who wants to date a girl for her money?" Jimmy asked. "I mean, she was pretty hot, but that's all she had going for her."

"You're saying you broke up with her because, why?" Nicky asked, not getting it, but this guy definitely seemed like a shithead if she'd ever seen one.

"I'm saying I broke up with her because she was boring," Jimmy said. "We had nothing in common. I wanted to go to the movies; she wanted to go to some party. We never got to do anything fun. But I didn't know she was dead. Damn..."

Nicky wasn't buying it. Jimmy barely seemed to care, and he and Frankie had dated for reportedly over a year. Even if she was "boring," would it kill him to shed a tear, or show any kind of remorse or care that she was dead? That in itself was enough for Nicky to look twice—a lack of empathy for others was a hallmark sign of a sociopath or psychopath, and Nicky felt damn sure that would fit the profile of the man she was hunting.

"Aren't you upset at all?" Nicky asked. "You dated for a long time, didn't you?"

"A little while, I guess," Jimmy said. "It was more serious for her than it was for me, I guess. Sorry if that makes me sound like a dick, but it is what it is."

Nicky exchanged a look with Ken. He nodded at her, and she knew what he was thinking. There was something wrong about Jimmy's reaction.

Nicky walked over and sat down on the arm of the couch, close to Jimmy.

"Look, Jimmy," she said. "I've been doing this job a long time, and I've learned that people are never as simple as they seem. Maybe you don't want to come across like a jerk, but the fact of the matter is, you're hiding something."

"I'm not hiding anything," Jimmy said, smiling. "I'm just saying that Frankie wasn't for me. I'm a simple guy. I like football, I like beer, and I like sex."

Ken snorted. "I'm sure you're a real catch."

Jimmy's face darkened. "What's that supposed to mean?"

But Nicky knew where this was going—Ken did this sometimes, got all rowdy with the male suspects, as it sometimes got them angry and got them to slip up. He could work that angle well, although it sometimes ended up getting more hostile.

"It means you're a shit, Jimmy," Ken said. "Francine was a nice girl, but you treated her like garbage. And now she's dead. What are we supposed to do with that information, Jimmy?"

"Huh?" He looked between them. "What the hell do you mean, man?"

Nicky glanced to her right. Through the kitchen window, in the backyard, she could see it:

A Hana Kuma car, parked at the back of the yard.

There it was.

Her jaw tight, she looked up at Jimmy, who wrung his hand along the back of his neck.

"We hear you own a Hana Kuma car, yes?" Nicky said. "We're looking for a vehicle just like that."

"Huh?" Jimmy went pale, and he moved aside, as if to block Nicky and Ken from seeing out the window in the back. "I don't have a car like that."

Nicky slipped off of the couch and walked over to the window. Jimmy stepped aside, shaking, and she looked out. There was no mistaking the car that was parked in the yard. It was a Hana Kuma car. The same model, the same color. The same rusted, dented doors and the same cracked windows.

"Then what's--"

Something crashed behind her, and Nicky whirled around to see Jimmy--making a run for the front door.

"Lyons!" Ken shouted, diving after Jimmy. He hit the man, and they both went tumbling to the floor. Jimmy struggled to get up, and Ken struggled to hold him down. On the couch, Nicky grabbed for the phone and dialed the local PD.

"We've got a 10-15," she said. "3313--"

Jimmy broke free from Ken, who fell over, and Jimmy ran for the back door. He grabbed the door handle, but something was stopping him from opening it.

"Jimmy Drake, this is the FBI!" Ken shouted. "You will not leave--"

Jimmy was fast, but Ken was faster. He caught Jimmy and tackled him to the floor, pinning him down and handcuffing him.

Jimmy struggled against Ken's weight, but Ken didn't budge an inch.

"You have the right to remain silent," Ken said, calmly. "Anything you say can and will be used against you in a court of law. You have the right to an attorney--"

Jimmy began to scream. "No! No! I didn't do anything!"

Ken ignored him. "You have the right to an attorney. If you cannot afford one, one will be provided for you. Do you understand these rights as they have been read to you?"

Jimmy screamed again, and he kept struggling. Nicky hurried to Ken's side, and helped him put Jimmy in cuffs.

"I didn't kill her!" Jimmy screamed. "I didn't do anything!"

"Then you have nothing to worry about," Ken said, hauling Jimmy to his feet.

CHAPTER NINE

Nicky stood in front of the Hana Kuma sedan in Jimmy Drake's backyard. A crew of police officers swarmed the house, while Jimmy himself was being held in handcuffs by an officer in the backyard. Nicky wanted him close by as they searched for more evidence of his guilt--photos, items that could belong to the girls, anything. And Nicky wanted to be the one to search the car first.

She looked over her shoulder to see Ken pass by inside the house--he was helping some other officers search Jimmy's property. With black gloves on, so as not to disturb any evidence, Nicky stepped closer to the car, ready to dig inside.

The first thing Nicky did was open the door to the front seat and search around. She opened the glove box, but there was nothing of note other than a lighter and a pack of cigarettes. She flipped through the papers and user manuals in the glovebox, shaking them out, but she found no photos. She moved to the back seat and patted it down, but still, no hint at the photos.

Then she moved to the trunk. As she lifted the lid and peered inside, her heart skipped a beat. There, sitting right in the middle of the trunk, was a bundle. The bundle was large and rectangular, with long, smooth edges. It was wrapped in plastic and secured with duct tape, and its contents glinted silver in the sunlight. Nicky sensed danger radiating from the bundle, hinting at its illicit nature.

This was evidence of not a small drug deal--but a major one.

Nicky looked over at Jimmy, who was being held by an officer at the back of his house. He was trembling as he watched Nicky with horror.

He knew he'd been caught.

Nicky nodded at the group of officers standing by for her, and they understood the signal to take over the gutting of the car. Nicky had other plans. She walked right up to Jimmy, who avoided her eyes as the officer held him with his hands behind his back.

"That's a lot of cocaine, Jimmy," Nicky said.

"It's--it's not mine, I swear," Jimmy stuttered.

"You know we don't believe that." Nicky propped a hand on her hip.

Jimmy shook his head, looking to his side at the officer holding him. "I didn't do anything, I swear! Those drugs aren't mine, man! I'm just holding them, I--"

"Save it, shit bag," the officer said, and Jimmy shut right up.

But something wasn't adding up to Nicky. Was this why he'd lied about the car? She didn't find any photos, or anything that proved Jimmy was the killer. But plenty of proof he was a drug dealer.

"Did Frankie know you were a drug dealer?" Nicky asked. "Is that why you killed her?"

"What?" Jimmy exclaimed. "I told you, I never hurt Frankie or anyone! Those drugs, I'm just... I'm just holding them!"

"We'll see," Nicky said. "If you don't want to tell us the truth, fine. We'll find it out."

"I didn't do anything!" Jimmy exclaimed again.

"You want to tell us where the rest of the photos are?" Nicky asked. "We'll find them, Jimmy. You know that. All you're doing is wasting our time and yours. The sooner you confess, the sooner we can get this over with."

"What photos?" Jimmy asked. "I don't have any photos!"

"Come on, you don't want to make this harder on yourself," Nicky sighed. She didn't have time for this.

"I don't have the photos!"

"Where are the photos?"

"I don't have any photos!" Jimmy protested. "I don't know anything about any photos, I swear!"

"Well, we'll have to scc about that," Nicky said, and she turned away. As she walked back to the house, she watched as the officers began to take apart the car. She had no time to waste on Jimmy. Not if she wanted to get to the bottom of this case before her time ran out.

Maybe Ken had better luck with the search inside the house. Nicky went in through the back door, where she was met with Jimmy's messy kitchen. The kitchen reeked of rotten food and uncleanliness, with the distinct scent of stale smoke and unwashed dishes. It was a mess, with dirty utensils strewn across the countertops, mounds of crumbs collecting on the floor, and smudges of grease and grime covering nearly every surface. Nicky grimaced as she stepped inside, wrinkling her nose at the overwhelming smell of dirt and decay. A few officers moved past her, and Nicky spotted Ken directing two more of them in the living room.

She stepped into the living room, where she spotted an officer kneeling beside a bookshelf. Nicky walked closer, and when she passed him, she saw the bottom of the bookshelf was lined with old photos. But they weren't Polaroids; they were just prints.

"Hey, be careful with those." Ken approached them. "Those are evidence."

"I am being careful," the officer said. "But it doesn't seem like any of these photos have anything to do with the ones we're looking for."

"Maybe not, but if we find one that we need, it could have fingerprints," Ken said. "And maybe a date stamp. You never know."

"So, I can take these?" the officer asked.

"Yes," Ken said. "Just be careful with them. They're important."

The officer tucked the photos into a folder, and he stood up. He moved away from the bookshelf, and Nicky went to look at the shelf where he had been kneeling. It was filled with old photos, some of them falling to the floor and collecting in a pile. They were all from Jimmy's family, from Christmas, birthdays, and other family get-togethers. There were photos of Jimmy's parents, his brothers, his grandparents. Even photos of Jimmy himself, as a young child, and then as a young teen. Nicky couldn't imagine him ever being young and innocent.

Ken finally noticed Nicky and looked over. "Hey, you're here."

"What did you find?" she asked.

"A lot of stuff," Ken said. "But nothing about the murders yet."

"Those aren't Polaroid pictures," Nicky noticed.

"No." Ken put his hands in his pockets and looked around the room. "And they're not incriminating either. I think they're from old family albums."

Even still, an affinity for photographs could make him a more desirable suspect.

"I found bricks of what I think is cocaine in his trunk," Nicky said, "but no photos, no Polaroid pictures."

"Damn," Ken said. "Guess that's what he was afraid of us finding."

"Yeah," Nicky muttered.

None of this was enough to one hundred percent pin these murders on Jimmy. But it was more than enough to bring him in for questioning.

***

The interrogation room was a small, windowless space with harsh florescent lighting. Nicky and Ken sat at a long table across from Jimmy, who sat in a metal chair with his arms crossed and his gaze fixed on the floor. The walls were bare, and the air felt tense and heavy with suspicion.

Jimmy slumped, defeated, in the chair, and he'd barely spoken more than one-word answers since they got into the interrogation room.

"You might as well start being honest with us, Jimmy," Nicky said, losing her patience. "You knew Frankie. You have the same car we're looking for. And we already found pounds of cocaine in your trunk."

"I didn't kill anyone," he said, "and I didn't take any pictures."

"Then what were you doing with the car?" Nicky asked.

"I'm not gonna talk about that," he said. "I don't want to go back to jail."

Nicky sighed and she leaned forward, putting her hands on the table. "You know what, Jimmy? I'll make a deal with you. You tell me what I want to know, and I'll make sure you're out of here."

"You won't find anything in that car," he said. "I'm telling you; I don't have any pictures."

"Did you take them to other antique stores?" Nicky asked, hoping that the curveball might make him react. But he didn't. He kept sulking.

"What stores, man?"

"The antique store where you planted the photos." Nicky leaned forward on the table. They'd wasted enough time trying to get him to fess up--it was time to lay all the cards down. "You drove your car to Harriet Antiques on August 18th, Jimmy. We have the security footage. We saw your car, and we can place it at the scene, so if you didn't take the photos, where did they come from and why did you plant them?"

Jimmy lifted his head, a bewildered look on his face, and for a moment Nicky thought maybe he was ready to fess up. But then he said, "Wait... August 18th?"

"Yes, Jimmy," Ken said. "You know what you did on that date."

"I do! And I wasn't in any damn antique shop!"

Nicky and Ken exchanged a glance.

"Go on," Nicky said.

"I was at work, man," he said. "You can get the security footage from my boss. At Greg's Auto Body back in Stoneycreek. I worked day and night that day after I fucked up on someone's car. I was there all day, man. I wasn't where you think I was."

Nicky didn't like the sound of that. If Jimmy really had an alibi--and they could confirm it with security footage--then that would clear him. But it would be a preposterous coincidence. The Hana Kuma car was rare, and Jimmy's model was the same as the one they were looking for.

They'd already proven that he was in possession of the same model of car, and he had cocaine in his trunk. Even if he had a perfect alibi, there was no way he wasn't involved...

But if he wasn't, then they were wasting time on him, and the real killer was still out there--potentially with another victim.

She leaned back in her chair and folded her arms. "We'll get the security footage," Nicky said. "You won't be going anywhere for a while."

"C'mon, man, the drugs weren't mine," Jimmy sputtered. "Let me go!"

But Nicky and Ken were already standing. Nicky couldn't waste another second on this guy. They had to confirm his alibi. But even if it checked out, Jimmy wasn't going anywhere for a long time--not with that much cocaine in his possession.

"Sorry, Jimmy," Ken said as they made their way to the door. "End of the road."

CHAPTER TEN

She was getting it all wrong. As she tried to contort her body into the pose he wanted, he seethed with anger at seeing the awkward angles she produced.

"No, no, not like that!" he yelled. "My camera would fucking break if I took photos of you looking like that!"

She whimpered like a pathetic, scared mutt. In his basement studio, he had everything perfect: the lighting, the mood, the set. He was going for a vintage, pinup style, but this woman--who he had trusted to be his perfect model--was failing him.

"Please," she begged, standing upright in front of the couch, "l-let me go, please."

"You will pose for me," he said through gritted teeth. "And you will do it right. Try again."

He held his camera up to her, and she sat back down, trying to cross her legs the way he'd wanted.

"Good," he said. "Now arch your back. Give the camera a smile."

With a pained, uncomfortable look, she managed to arch her back, pushing her chest forward and opening her mouth into something that resembled a smile.

"No," he said. "Too wide. Try it again."

As she tried to arch her back again, he took a step closer to her, and then another, until he was right behind her.

"Oh," she said, trying to scoot away from him. "Okay."

He grabbed her shoulder with one hand, holding the camera with the other.

"Oh, no, no, no," he said. "I need you to stay still."

"I'm not comfortable with it," she said, shaking her head. "Please, don't."

He gripped her shoulder tighter, the soft skin underneath his fingertips.

"I need you to trust me," he said. "I need you to do this right."

"I--"

He gripped her shoulders even tighter, his fingers digging into her soft flesh.

"Let me help you," he said. "Let me show you how to pose."

He sat down on the couch beside her and arched his body into the perfect pose. She watched him with fear in her eyes. He looked at her, so she'd know he wasn't messing around here.

"Like this," he said. "You will try it again."

He stood up and walked back over to his position.

She did as he asked, and he watched as her face contorted with a smile he had never seen before. He snapped a quick photo, and the flash brightened the room for a moment. He watched as the print came out of the Polaroid and slowly processed. It was mediocre. If this woman couldn't deliver them, he'd go get another one.

He thought back to the last model he had photographed: a soft-spoken, but sexy woman who had been happy to pose for him (with a little encouragement, of course). She had been art compared to this one.

He remembered the last moment he saw her, before he slit her throat and did her final photoshoot. It was perfect. What had her name been again? Francesca? Something like that.

No matter. He had replaced her with this new model, but she was proving to be quite the disappointment. If she didn't get him a good photo soon, he'd have to get rid of her and find a new model even sooner than planned.

He might have to kill this one and get her out of his hair.

"Try again?" she asked.

He nodded, and she stood back up, and this time, managed to pose right. She even managed to get the right look for him.

He snapped a photo, and then another. The flash lit the room up for a moment, and the print slowly started to appear.

"Good," he said. "Switch feet."

He watched as she tried to switch her feet, but it was sloppy.

"No," he said, frustrated. "Just stay facing the camera. Switch from your left foot to your right."

He watched as she tried again and again, and each time, she was still screwing it up.

"This isn't working!" he yelled. "You're fucking it all up!"

"P-please, I'll try again!" she said.

He walked up to her and grabbed her by her chin.

"Listen to me," he said, "I'm not keeping you here to give me mediocre photos. You're going to do this right, or else."

He could see she was scared. He could tell she knew he wasn't kidding.

"I want you to show me you're worth my time," he said. "I want you to give me a reason to keep you around."

He grabbed her by her hair and pulled her head back, exposing her neck.

"I can't do this without you on my side," he said. "I need you to show me that you're trying. Show me that you can do this."

He let go of her hair, and she turned around to face him.

"Okay," she said. "I'll try again."

"Good," he said, turning away. "Let's start again, from the top." He turned his camera on her. "This time, there will be no mistakes." A smile curled at his lips. "Or else this will be the last photoshoot you ever do."

CHAPTER ELEVEN

Nicky crossed her arms as she leaned back in the chair in the briefing room at the Stoneycreek police station, footage open on her laptop in front of her. Ken sat beside her, also sinking in his chair, because what they were looking at was definitive proof that Jimmy Drake did not leave those photos at the antique store.

It was grainy security footage of the auto body shop where he worked, and sure enough, it captured Jimmy at the exact time the other man had been seen dropping the photos. To be absolutely sure, Nicky skimmed through the footage again--but she knew that this was more than enough to clear him.

"Well, we have him on drug charges, anyway," Ken said, sighing.

Nicky clenched her teeth and closed her laptop. "Damn it."

All that time wasted and for nothing. It was getting late now, descending into evening, and the two FBI agents still had no leads. Nicky rubbed her eyes with her palms, taking comfort in the momentary darkness.

The pictures of those girls' slaughtered bodies in the photographs flashed in front of her eyes. The sheer violence of it all... it made Nicky sick. She could only imagine the type of deranged maniac who would do such a thing. Murder women, take pictures of them, and leave them somewhere public for any innocent person to find.

It was... it was heinous.

Ken cleared his throat, standing up. "I'm gonna grab some coffee. You want anything?"

Nicky shook her head, still staring at the table. "I'm good, thanks."

She heard her partner walk away. As soon as Ken was gone, she stood up and began to pace the room. Her mind was racing, trying to think of something, anything, they could do to catch this guy.

The fact that they couldn't find any connection between any of the victims was troubling. It made predicting who he might take next even more difficult. They were all pretty, brown-haired girls, but there had to be something more than that. Another issue was, they had no idea where he would even strike next. If Paris was taken from Miami, and

Francine from here, in Northern Florida, then this guy clearly had a huge reach. He wasn't afraid to travel.

And he did have the car. It had no license plate, but it was a somewhat unique make. Maybe Nicky's only hope now was to try to track that car--or a car like it. But it discouraged her, because they'd already tried that route with the car, and it had led them to a dead end.

But she had to try. Pacing across the room, Nicky called Grace. As usual, the tech picked up within a ring.

"Hey, Nicky, how's it going?"

"Not so good, Grace," Nicky said. "Jimmy Drake's not our guy."

"Ah, shit! Sorry to hear that--he seemed like the right one for sure."

"It's a different car. But we know for sure that the person who dropped off the photos did drive a Hana Kuma. We also know he's potentially driven all across Florida. I was hoping you could help me track this car down."

"Without a license plate?"

Nicky swallowed. "That's right. We're looking for a Hana Kuma with no license plate."

"That might not be easy to get on security footage," Grace said. It was the first time Nicky had heard her hesitate. Normally, Grace was right on top of things, but Nicky knew this could be a wild goose chase.

"I know it's a lot to ask, Grace," Nicky said. "If you can, recover traffic footage from across the state and see what you can find. Try Miami, around the time Paris went missing."

"Nicky, this is a really big request."

"I know," Nicky said, running her fingers up and down her hair. "But if we get this guy, this will all be worth it."

Grace was silent for a moment. "Okay, Nicky," she said. "I'll do what I can. Just give me some time."

"Thanks, Grace."

Nicky hung up, feeling a weight lifted off of her shoulders. If there was even a chance that Grace could find this car, then she was going to take it. And she would find this guy, whoever he was.

Nicky just needed something to go her way.

But she knew firsthand how impossible it could be to track a vehicle with no identification. She knew because when she and her sister had been kidnapped all those years ago, all Nicky had for the officers was a description of the van they'd been in. No license plate number.

And it had never been found, to this day.

Nicky remembered it so clearly, too. The make… the build… but it had been no help. There were simply too many of them in America—in the world—and without a plate, it was impossible to narrow down who could've taken them. Nicky would love to take a look again, with the resources of the FBI behind her, but of course, she didn't have permission to do that yet.

If she could get Felix to talk, or get information out of him, then she would have something, though. She had to have something.

Nerves tore through her. No... she couldn't think like that. She had to stay resolute. For the victims. And for Rosie.

Nicky began to pace again, even as Ken arrived with two cups of coffee. "I know you said you didn't want one," he said, "but I got you one anyway."

"Thanks, Ken." Nicky took the cup and sipped it, feeling the warm liquid flow down her throat. It was strong and bitter, but it was comforting to have. "I just talked to Grace," she said. "She's going to try to recover any traffic footage from around Miami, around the time Paris went missing."

"And she can do that?"

"If she can't, I don't know who can," Nicky said. Her footsteps slowed to a halt, and she turned to face Ken. "I just don't know what else we can do to track this guy. There's no forensic data on the photographs. And we still don't even know where the bodies are."

"True," Ken said. "He could've put those girls anywhere."

Nicky sat back down at the table and pulled out the files, taking out the print-offs of the Polaroid photos. She looked at them closely, for any identifying mark in the background, but it was completely non-descript. It looked to be a basement of some kind, with concrete flooring. In the background of one photo, she could see a vintage floral couch. On the photo with the chair, the girl was sitting, slumped, on another vintage-style chair.

"He seems to have old furniture," Nicky noted.

Ken sat down next to her with his coffee, looking over the photos. "Yeah, they don't make them like that anymore."

"And he dropped the photos in an antique store," Nicky said.

"So, what," Ken began, "You think we're looking for an antique fanatic?"

"Maybe," Nicky said. "Or an older person, who was alive when this style was popular." She shook her head. "I don't know. It's just a theory."

"You could be onto something," Ken said. "The Polaroid photo--that's a vintage thing too."

Nicky allowed her mind to wander, building up a profile of this person in her mind. They knew he had an affinity for photography. For vintage photography, at that, and vintage furniture. He obviously wanted his photographs to be seen, as he came in and planted them himself.

That meant he was confident--he didn't want to spend the rest of his life in prison. But he was also meticulous, as he'd driven all across Florida to do this.

"It's hard to believe he's just some random guy," Ken said. "That he just happened to carry a camera and decided to take these photos. He's obviously the type of person who would have been wanting to do something like this for a long time. Someone doesn't just wake up and become this."

Nicky nodded, sitting back, her mind whirring. Talking to Ken was helping her to work it out in her mind. "I know," she said. "I was thinking about the same thing. Like he wants to be seen. But something about it seems off. We know that these girls didn't know each other, that they'd never met. The victims are from completely different parts of the state. And the murders appear to be completely random. And the photographs..." She took a breath, unsure where her mind was leading her. She was onto something--she just wasn't sure what yet.

Just then, Nicky's phone rang. She snatched it off the table, but it was an unknown number.

"This is Agent Lyons," Nicky said into the phone.

"Agent Lyons? This is Officer Green with the Cedar Bay PD--I was given your contact information by Chief Gammage of the Pine Grove PD."

Nicky's heart picked up. "Yes, that's right. Can I help you?"

"I was told to call you personally if we found any evidence of any disturbing photographs in our town," he said, and Nicky's eyes flashed to Ken. He mirrored her expression.

"Did you find some?" she asked, her heart in her throat.

"Actually, we did," he said. "We found a photo of what appears to be a female homicide victim in an antique store here in our town."

Nicky stood up, clutching the phone so tightly she thought the plastic might crack. "What antique store?" she asked.

"It's called Olden's Antiques," he said, "right here in Cedar Bay."

Nicky froze, and then started to breathe rapidly. "Where in the store? Where exactly?"

"It was by the cash register, mixed into a pile of old photographs and postcards. The owner said he didn't see it until the police came in looking."

"When did this happen?"

"About twenty minutes ago. We're processing the scene now. I was told to contact you by Chief Gammage."

"Thanks, Officer Green," Nicky said. "I'm on my way."

She hung up and faced Ken. This was huge, but not necessarily in a good way.

It meant there was a third victim--a third woman who had lost her life. But it also gave them another scene, another clue to chase down, which would hopefully lead them to the killer and stop him from claiming anyone else.

But they had another body. Another photo. She knew that it was a woman, but there was no way of knowing for sure what the circumstances were surrounding her death.

Only one thing was certain. This guy was escalating. And he wasn't about to stop.

CHAPTER TWELVE

Nicky couldn't stop trembling as she drove her car toward the small town of Cedar Bay, over an hour away from Stoneycreek. Evening was descending upon them, and plumes of pink and orange took over the sky as it darkened, the sun dipping over the Florida horizon.

"It's going to be okay," Ken said from the passenger seat. "We'll get him, whoever he is."

Nicky nodded. She was so nervous she could barely speak, but she knew she had to try. She had to keep going--for those girls.

She'd gotten in touch with Officer Green, who was going to meet them at the scene. Now, she was driving as quickly as she could across the state, trying to keep her thoughts in order.

"I can't believe he's been leaving evidence behind," she said. "It's like he wants to us to chase him."

"Yeah, it's hard to imagine how these sickos really think," Ken said. "Back when I was training to be an agent, one of the hardest things for me was to get into the mindset of the killer. It's disturbing stuff."

"But necessary for our jobs," Nicky said. "Otherwise, we'd never be able to catch them."

"Yeah, yeah," Ken said. "But that doesn't mean I have to like it."

It was true, though—getting into the mind of a killer was never easy.

Nicky was quiet, letting her mind whir, trying to piece together the clues they had. It was clear that this guy was smart--but he was also cocky. He'd dropped the photos in an antique store, but they'd ended up in the hands of police. It was inevitable they would, and surely he knew that.

"I mean, all these girls--we have no idea what he's doing with them," Nicky continued, ranting more than anything else. "They're just gone. And we can't find them. We don't even have their bodies, just those horrible pictures."

"That's the hardest part," Ken said. "But we will, Nicky. He's going to slip up. He's going to make a mistake. And we'll be there to catch him."

Nicky nodded, but she knew that there was a high chance that the man they were looking for was smart. And the thought of that scared her the most. The thought that he was smart enough to evade them long enough to kill one, two, maybe even three more victims before getting caught.

Nicky couldn't handle that amount of blood on her hands. They'd already lost too many. If Nicky didn't crack this case in good time, she feared that the task force would be declared a failure—and she would be a consequence of that. This whole task force was Nicky's shot to prove she could get results with as few deaths as possible. If she continued to fail, maybe they'd put someone else in charge, or axe it altogether.

The thought made her stomach bottom out. No… she had to prove herself. Nicky's destiny was the FBI, and she did want to advance. Maybe even become Special Agent someday. Special Agent Nicky Lyons… she liked the sound of that.

But she'd never get there if she gave up.

Nicky's mind wandered as she drove, her exhaustion taking over. As she saw the small town go by out her window, she thought about those girls, their lives cut short.

She thought of the man who'd done that to them, who'd taken their lives. She thought of what they were going through. And she knew, with a deep sense of conviction, that they were going to stop him.

In her mind, she could see them. The three women, their lives snuffed out in an instant. She could see the man who'd taken them, who'd killed them. His face was blurry, but Nicky knew she could pull it into focus.

She wasn't going to stop. Even if she never got promoted, even if her task force did get snuffed out—she had to fight for these girls.

She wanted to be the one to catch that bastard.

She drove faster, and the trees sped by her in a blur of green and brown, the sun setting as they approached Cedar Bay.

Nicky knew that there was a chance they'd be approaching the scene and find absolutely nothing. No facial ID, no fingerprints. But she still had to see it for herself.

They came into the small, quaint beachside town of Cedar Bay. Nicky's car weaved through the narrow, winding roads. The quaint shops and restaurants were nestled between rows of tightly packed houses and dotted with colorful beach umbrellas. Buildings shimmered in the evening sun as she drove, reflecting ripples of light across the quiet streets. The salty ocean breeze blew gently in Nicky's face through the open window, carrying with it the faint scent of salt, seaweed, and damp sand.

Finally, as it was getting darker, they pulled into the parking lot of Olden's Antiques. Nicky could see other police vehicles there, and her heart started to beat faster.

She parked and got out of the car, and Ken followed her. The two of them headed toward the store, and one officer--a young, tall, lanky man--waved at them. Nicky and Ken held up their badges.

"Agent Lyons?" the officer asked, and Nicky recognized his voice.

"You must be Officer Green," she said.

"That's right. Thanks so much for coming so quickly. The manager of the store is inside," Officer Green said. "He's been really upset about this. I think he's on the edge of a breakdown."

"I understand," Nicky said. "Thanks for calling us."

Officer Green nodded, and then they headed into the store. The lights were dim, casting the store in a gloomy darkness. Nicky looked around the store and frowned. She couldn't even see the stack of photographs the officer had told her about. The store was filled with old and dusty furniture, with pieces sprawling haphazardly across the floor. The air was thick with the musty smell of old fabrics, carved wood, and tarnished metal. The shelves were lined with rare and valuable antiques, glittering in the dim light.

Officer Green led them to the back of the store, where the cash register was, and a man--the manager--was being spoken to by two other officers.

"We have forensics standing by," Officer Green told them. "But you can see everything for yourself back here."

They approached the register, where the manager--a distraught-looking older man--looked at them.

"Oh, is that the FBI?" he asked.

"Yes, sir," Nicky said. "I'm Agent Lyons and this is Agent Walker. Where was the photograph located?"

He nodded at a pile next to him. Nicky pulled out a glove and slid it on.

On top of the pile was a picture, a Polaroid, just like the others. This one showed a young woman in a blue dress, slumped on a couch, with her throat slit, blood leaking everywhere, all over the furniture.

Nicky's stomach twisted. She looked at the picture and felt rage rise up in her like a tidal wave. She wanted to find this man.

"We'll need to talk to you about this," Nicky said to the manager.

"Okay," the manager said, but he didn't sound okay. His voice and hands were shaking. He looked as if he was on the verge of collapse.

"We already questioned him a lot," Green cut in. "He doesn't seem to know anything."

Nicky focused on the manager. "You have no idea who could have placed this here, or when?"

"I don't know! People rarely look at that pile, if ever. It's mostly for decoration. We have old photographs and postcards, and it's all for fun, really. When the police came in and said they were looking for something, I didn't expect them to actually find anything."

"I understand," Nicky said. "And you have surveillance footage in the store?"

"I don't," he said. "We... we don't have a lot of crime in town. At all. So, you can imagine how shocking this is for me."

Nicky nodded, though she was still frowning. She turned to Officer Green.

"We're going to need you to get footage from the streets as soon as you can," she said. "Look for a 1998 Hana Kuma. We have reason to believe the culprit may be driving that vehicle."

"I will," he said. "But we get a lot of tourists here, and people often wander in and out. It's mostly quiet, so there's not a lot of motion. You might not even be able to see the person who dropped that photograph off."

"Well, we need to try," she said. "You might as well call forensics in and take this man home for the night. He doesn't need to endure this any longer."

"Oh, thank you," the manager said.

"We're on it," Officer Green said.

With that, the manager left with the officers, leaving Nicky and Ken alone to survey the scene. Nicky set the photo back down, looking closely at it to see if there was another detail. The girl, like the others, had brown hair and was young and pretty. But the scene was a bit different too. The angle was wider. They could see more of the background.

Squinting, Nicky looked even closer. It was too dark. Nicky took out her phone and snapped a photo, then, on her phone, she went into the picture settings and upped the brightness, turning the screen to Ken.

There was a texture in the background.

No, not a texture--a wallpaper.

Damask. Blue and yellow in color. Something about it was familiar.

"We've seen this before," Nicky said to Ken.

He frowned at the screen. "Yeah, we have..."

But where? Why was it so familiar?

Then, it hit her:

"Mr. Dumond," Nicky said.

"What?" Ken frowned.

Her heart raced. No--she was certain of it. They'd seen that wallpaper earlier that day--at Harriet Antique. "It was in Mr. Dumond's shop," Nicky said. "He had this wallpaper at his store."

"Shit," Ken said. "He did. But he was so nice. We can't actually think..."

"I don't know. But we need to look into him."

***

Back in the car, Nicky had her laptop open while Ken sat in the passenger seat. Her fingers clacked at the keyboard as she searched for Charles Dumond from Pine Grove... but nothing came up.

"He said he'd lived there his whole life, didn't he?" Nicky asked. "He's not in the database."

"Maybe there are other Charles Dumonds, not from Pine Grove?" Ken offered.

Nicky checked that. The sun had fully set now, and they were sitting in the car, the only brightness coming from the screen. The police were still working at the store across from them, looking for more evidence, but Nicky had a strong feeling they'd find none.

"There are other Charles Dumonds, but nonc who seem related to him," Nicky said, scrolling through a list of names and photos. "These aren't him."

"So, it's an alias," Ken said. "He lied to us."

"It would appear that way," Nicky said. "But why would he lie? Why would someone who runs an antique store lie about where he lives and who he is?"

"Well, if he's the one who's been planting these photographs," Ken said, "he lied to make himself look innocent."

That was a very good point.

"It seems that way," Nicky said. She wasn't sure why, but she didn't want to believe it. Mr. Dumond had been such a kind man.

But who was he, really?

Nicky went online and looked up Harriet Antique, and what came up was an article from Pine Grove--with a picture of Mr. Dumond, smiling, looking kind as always. But they had a photo of him--which meant they might be able to track down his real ID.

"Before we go in guns blazing," Nicky said, "we need to know who we're dealing with. I bet Grace can track him down. I'll give her a call."

She pulled out her phone and dialed Grace's number. Grace picked up on the third ring.

"Hey, Nicky," Grace said. "Sorry, I'm still looking into--"

"Forget the car for now," Nicky said. "I'm sending you a photo of a man who might be living in Pine Grove under an alias. Think you can find out who he is?"

"I can run his face through the system and see if we get a match, yeah," Grace said.

"Good. Forwarding it now."

With a few clicks, Nicky saved the photo and sent it to Grace's email. She waited with bated breath for Grace to accept.

"Okay, got it," Grace said. "Running him through the system now. Let's see if we get a match..."

Moments passed. Nicky heard Grace's keyboard clacking on the other end of the line.

Then, finally, Grace said:

"I got a hit. His name is Richard Fanson. Seventy-one years old. Born in Brooklyn, New York."

Nicky's head spun. Richard Fanson from New York. That was nothing close to Charles Dumond from Pine Grove, Florida.

"Send me everything we have on him," Nicky said.

"Will do."

She hung up the phone and turned to Ken. But her heart was pounding. To think, they could have already had the killer right in their sights all along...

"We're close," she said. "I know it. I just don't know how close."

"It's hard to believe," he said. "He seemed so nice."

"I know," she said. "That's what everyone always says about serial killers."

They were quiet for a moment, reflecting on that.

"We showed him the pictures," Ken said. "He knew something was wrong. He knew what they were."

"He did," Nicky said. "On some level, he did."

Nicky's computer dinged--a message from Grace. She'd forwarded some key documents on Richard Fanson, aka, Mr. Dumond.

Diagnosed with schizophrenia, he had been in and out of psychiatric hospitals his entire life. Not only that--but he had a criminal record.

Nicky paged through the documents, her stomach sinking.

The more she read, the worse it got.

A string of charges going back to when he was in his twenties: assault, robbery, a few misdemeanors. If he was the one, then that would mean the sketchy man seen with the Hana Kuma had nothing to do with this.

Nicky's heart raced. "He could be the one," she said. "He could be our guy."

"But if he's spent his life in and out of hospitals, how did he end up at an antique store?" Ken asked.

"It's hard to say," she said. "Maybe he's not as bad as he was. Maybe he hasn't committed a crime in a long time. Maybe... maybe these photos are making him act out again."

Ken looked at her. "So, what do we do?"

She drew a breath, then shut her laptop, tossed it in the back, and turned the car on. "We pay him another visit."

CHAPTER THIRTEEN

Nicky parked her car in front of Harriet Antiques, where the lights were on inside--and they could see Mr. Dumond behind the counter. Ken had called ahead and asked if he could come back down to the shop to meet them so they could look for further evidence, and without hesitation, Mr. Dumond had obliged.

Now, he was inside waiting for them. But Nicky was deep in thought, trying to work out what she thought was true and what wasn't. She tried to put herself in the position of Mr. Dumond--who seemed like a kind, old man, but who also might be a serial killer. It was difficult to reconcile the two ideas.

She and Ken got out. The sun had long since set over Pine Grove, but there were still cars to be seen, and people going about their business. Someone was walking a dog, and a few people were going into and out of the local bar. It was a quaint, peaceful town to live in, and Nicky might understand why an old man with a long history of mental illness would want to retire here. But did he really come here to start a killing spree? Was a seventy-one-year-old man capable of these heinous crimes?

Nicky didn't know. But she did know they had enough circumstantial evidence to bring him in for questioning.

And now, they had a name, too. They had a photo. They had a record. They had everything they needed. And if they could get him to confess, they might be able to move on this case once and for all.

But Nicky didn't know how to go about this. She didn't want to come on too aggressively and freak him out.

"Here's our game plan," Nicky told Ken. "We won't tip him off that we know anything is up with him at first, just prod and ask questions, and see how he reacts. We don't want to spook him."

"Agreed," Ken said. "If he's as unhinged as his file suggests... we don't want him to blow a gasket on us."

They got out of the car, into the warm night, and walked up to the store. Ken opened the door to the shop and went inside, and Nicky followed close behind. Mr. Dumond rose from behind the counter, a smile on his face.

"You're back!" he said.

"We are," Nicky said. "Thank you for coming in."

She glanced at the wallpaper. It was definitely the same as the wallpaper in the photo. Or, at the very least, extremely similar.

"I'm happy to help," Mr. Dumond said. "Please, sit down."

Nicky and Ken went to the table and sat down, and Mr. Dumond sat across from them. It seemed strange to Nicky to be talking to someone who might be a serial killer. She looked him over--calm, collected, friendly. It was hard to believe.

"I'm sure you're aware of the situation," Ken said.

Mr. Dumond nodded. "Yes, I am," he said. "I saw the news earlier. They found a photograph in another town. I guess my shop isn't the only victim of this crime."

"Right," Nicky said. "Unfortunately, we haven't ID'd the photographer yet, but we wanted to know if you could tell us anything about the type of Polaroid camera he was using. You have a lot of vintage cameras here, so maybe you can give us some insight on the make and model."

Mr. Dumond frowned. "Well, I'm not sure if I'm the best person to ask. I have quite the collection, but I'm not an expert on any of this. I'm sure you could ask a collector for a more informed opinion."

Nicky looked at Ken. She wasn't sure why, but there was something about his reluctance to answer the question that made her suspicious. It was almost as if he was hiding something.

"So, you don't know the brand of camera?" Nicky said.

"Not at all," he said. "I'm terribly sorry. I wish I could help."

"You're sure you don't know anything else about the culprit?" Nicky asked.

"I'm afraid not," Mr. Dumond said. "But I wish I could help." He looked down, genuinely sad. "I wish I could be of more use."

"Well, you've lived here a long time," Ken said. "Do you know of anyone in town who has an interest in these types of cameras?"

"Hmm, well, as I told you before, we get a lot of tourists, and I'm sure there are many photography enthusiasts in town."

Nicky looked around the shop as Ken asked questions, trying to spot anything suspicious, or any piece of furniture that might match something seen in the photos of the victims. But she saw nothing. The only connection was the wallpaper.

Maybe it was time to kick this up a notch.

"When did you have that wallpaper installed, Mr. Dumond?" Nicky asked.

"Hmm?" He looked around. "Oh... it was there when I bought the shop. The people who sold it to me said it had been there since before they had it too. It's an antique itself, you see."

"Right," Nicky said. "You said you lived here your whole life. Do you remember the different people who owned the shop before the people who sold it to you?"

"Oh, yes," he said. "I've been coming here for years. Before me, the owners were a husband and wife team from Canada. They had a string of failed antique stores before this one, and as soon as they moved in, they changed the name to 'Harriet Antiques.' I always liked that."

"Why?" Ken asked.

"I don't know," Mr. Dumond said. "I think it just has a nice ring to it. It's a bit more personalized than the other stores."

Nicky's ears perked up. "Can I ask why they moved here?" she said.

"Oh, I think they just needed a change," Mr. Dumond said. "Or maybe they just wanted a fresh start."

"Sometimes we all need a fresh start," Nicky said, her eyes flashing on Mr. Dumond's. "But if you've lived here your whole life, I suppose you wouldn't know about that."

Sweat pooled on Mr. Dumond's brow. "I suppose not..." He laughed uncomfortably. "I'm sorry, dears, I have to go to the washroom. When you get to my age, it gets harder to hold it in."

Nicky and Ken exchanged a look as Mr. Dumond got up and hobbled toward the back of the store. Once alone, Nicky whispered to Ken, "What do you think?"

"I think he's a practiced liar," he muttered.

That was true. And right now, everything was pointing at him. His shop was ground zero for the photographs...

Moments ticked on, and Mr. Dumond still did not return from the bathroom. Nicky felt her gut tighten with anticipation. She had to do something.

"Ken, I'm going to check on him," she said.

They got up from the table and went to the bathroom door. Ken knocked.

"Mr. Dumond?" he asked.

No reply.

He knocked on the door again. "Mr. Dumond?" he repeated.

Nicky turned the knob and slowly opened the door.

Mr. Dumond was nowhere to be seen.

The bathroom was a tiny little space. It didn't take long to search, but when they were done, they were still unable to find him. He had disappeared. He had left them all alone in the shop.

"Where the fuck is he?" Ken whispered. "There's no back door here."

"I don't know," Nicky said. "But we need to find him."

Ken was right--the shop had no back door, only a front, and they would have seen the old man sneak out. He had to be in here somewhere.

"Mr. Dumond?" Nicky called out. Carefully, they made their way through the store. "Are you in here? We're worried about you..."

"Come on out, Mr. Dumond," Ken echoed. "You don't need to hide from us. We're not gonna hurt you."

"Mr. Dumond?" Nicky said. "Please, we don't have time for this."

They searched the store from top to bottom. They found nothing, and they were only ones there.

She and Ken looked at each other. They had one last place to search.

The room behind the counter, where the computer had been. As they walked up to it, they realized the door was closed.

"Mr. Dumond?" Nicky called out. She knocked on the door. "Are you in there?"

No answer. But they couldn't waste time here. Nicky put her hand on her gun--just in case--and slowly opened the door.

Huddled in the corner of the room was Mr. Dumond--and he had an old musket pointed right at them.

"Shit!" Nicky ducked out of the way, bringing Ken with her--but the shot never came. Realizing Mr. Dumond hadn't fired the gun, Nicky took a breath to calm herself. She nodded at Ken, and they both took out their guns.

"Mr. Dumond," Ken said. "Drop your weapon and come out."

"N-no!" he shouted. "Who are you people, really? What do you want from me?"

"We just want to talk about the pictures, Mr. Dumond," Nicky said.

"No--you're... you're them, aren't you? You found me!"

"Who, Mr. Dumond?" Nicky asked. Ken shot her a confused frown too. "Are you running from someone, Mr. Dumond? Is that why you changed your name and moved here from New York?"

Silence.

But then, through the silence, something fell. Nicky turned her head and saw it--a forgotten bottle of pills. They had slipped out of Mr. Dumond's pocket.

"Mr. Dumond..." she said slowly. "Why did you move here?"

"I... I..." He was sweating. "My family... I had to get away... I had to..."

Nicky exchanged a look with Ken. They still didn't know what this was about, but they knew they had to get to the bottom of it.

"If someone is after you, Mr. Dumond," Ken said, "we can help you. But you gotta drop the gun."

"I can't!" he shouted. "You took away everything! I have nothing left! You killed everyone!"

"Mr. Dumond, we're... we're not..." Nicky struggled to find the right words. "We're not the people after you. If you're running from someone, then we can help you. But we need you to come out of there."

"No!" Mr. Dumond shouted. "You're lying! You are them! You killed him and you'll kill me too!"

"Who?" Nicky said. "Who did we kill, Mr. Dumond?"

"He was... he was the only one who'd ever been nice to me..." Mr. Dumond's words dissolved into tears.

"Who, Mr. Dumond?" Nicky said. "Who was it?"

She knew he had been diagnosed with schizophrenia, but this wasn't making any sense. Anxiety clawed through Nicky. She needed to end this now.

"Please drop the gun, Mr. Dumond," she said. "You don't want to hurt us. We're not your enemies."

For a moment, she thought he wasn't going to do it. But then, the gun started to shake.

"I... I... I..." Mr. Dumond stuttered. "I--"

Then he fainted, and the musket clattered to the floor.

Nicky heaved a sigh of relief. She and Ken ran to the other side of the counter and helped Mr. Dumond up.

"Are you alright, Mr. Dumond?" she said.

"I..." he stammered. "I'm fine..."

His eyes were open, his face pale. "I--I think I just blacked out for a bit."

Nicky almost felt bad for the guy. Maybe he was being honest—maybe he wasn't; it was impossible to say right now. Either way, they had him, and they needed to take him in.

"It's nice to see you awake again," Nicky said. "But I'm afraid we need you to come down to the station with us."

CHAPTER FOURTEEN

The dim light from his TV filled the room. The news was out. He couldn't believe it--his story was finally breaking. Finally, the world would see what he was worth.

He sat on the cold concrete floor of his basement in front of the old tube TV, biting his nail with his knees to his chest. On the screen, a news reporter:

"Several reports are coming in that somebody has been leaving photographs of homicide victims in antique stores," the woman said. "The photos, which are graphic in nature, appear to show actual victims, and police aren't sure who is taking them. Two victims have so far been identified as Paris Conner of Miami, Florida, and Francine Gibbons of Stoneycreek, Florida. A third victim has been photographed, but police have not yet identified her."

"Yes!" he exclaimed, smiling wildly. "Yes!"

He launched to his feet and danced around the studio, smiling gleefully.

"This is it! Finally, the cat is out of the bag... I can finally show you to the world, for real!"

He turned to the woman, lying slumped on his couch, with her throat slit. She looked so gorgeous in that red dress and had looked even better in the photoshoot he just completed. Alive, she had failed him.

But in death, she had proved to be a truly great model.

He took a deep breath.

"Now, it's time for my masterpiece."

The perfect image for his masterpiece.

He walked back to the girl and looked down at her. She was so beautiful there, lying on his couch with her throat slit, her blood pooling on the floor under her. He wished he could just leave her there, but as nice as that would be, it wasn't practical—she would start to rot, become stinky and fleshy and stain his wonderful couch, so the next subject would have their set ruined. No, this one, he had other plans for.

He turned back to the TV, where the reporter was still talking: "To date, police have no clues about who is taking the photos, or why. If you have any information about this case, please contact the police."

He laughed bitterly. "Oh, I will," he said. "I'll give them plenty of information. I'll give them a little clue..." He turned back to the woman on the couch.

It was time to move her.

She was surprisingly heavy, but he managed to throw her over his shoulder. He hauled her up the stairs. He knew just where he'd bring her--the perfect place to leave his mark. All he had to do was get her in his car, and then they would begin their final road trip together.

It was a warm, beautiful night, the perfect night to make his true debut. He threw her in the back of his car, and then climbed into the driver's seat. He started the engine, and then pulled out of the driveway and began to drive.

The woman's body was in the back seat. He smiled as he saw her in his rear view mirror.

"I'm so sorry, my dear. I know this isn't how you imagined your career would end, but you are my muse, and it's your duty to help me." He reached back and stroked her hair. "You will be remembered, my dear. You will be remembered."

He drove on.

He had his masterpiece in the back seat.

All he needed now was an audience.

It must have been an hour of driving under the hazy night sky, but it felt like a blur of euphoria and bliss. He breathed in deeply, listening to the lull of the car beneath him, thinking back to the days when he was invisible.

That would be no more.

His art teachers never appreciated him. They never saw his talent.

They never saw what he could do.

But soon, they would.

And they would be sorry they ever treated him like a nobody.

After all, he was finally going to get what he deserved.

He pulled into a largely-empty parking lot. He got out of his car, smiling, and then walked around to the back seat, where his model was still lying. He pulled his mask down over his face, so he didn't need to worry about being recognized.

"Come on, my dear," he said, pulling the woman's body out of the back seat.

He tossed her over his shoulder and looked around. It was late in town, no people around. This special shop was located on the outskirts of town, making it the perfect place to leave her, as there was no one around at this time, not even a dog walker.

The shop had long been closed. He looked up at the name of it and smiled. It was perfect! This would really leave his mark.

He went up the steps leading up to the store, then lay the girl down on the steps, letting her fall naturally into position. Yes, yes, that would do. There was no need to hide now.

He looked at her lying there, dressed in her red dress, her hair splayed out around her head.

"You will be one of my many masterpieces," he said. "The world will remember you, my dear. I promise you that."

He leaned down and kissed her on the lips.

"I promise you that."

He stood up and pulled out his camera, then started taking pictures.

She did look lovely like that, lying there on the steps, dressed in red.

He raised the camera to his face, smiling, and took pictures. Then, he removed one of the Polaroids from their earlier shoot. He went up to the doors of the shop and, wearing gloves so there'd be no mark of him left behind, he taped it to the door.

"You will be remembered, my dear," he said. "You will be remembered forever. And so will I. When they see you... they'll really be seeing me."

CHAPTER FIFTEEN

At the Pine Grove police station, Nicky and Ken sat across from a sad-looking Charles Dumond--whose real name was, of course, Richard Fanson. As suspicious as he was looking, Nicky couldn't help but feel bad for the old man slumped in the seat across from them, who had obviously been triggered by the entire situation.

Nicky's theory was that he realized they were onto him and snapped. But they couldn't, for sure, pin the murders on him. Not yet.

In a strange way... Nicky found herself hoping it *wasn't* him. That he was just an ill old man who ran away from a bad life in another place, then came here to start fresh. When talking to policemen, Nicky learned that the townspeople loved Mr. Dumond. It would be a tragedy to learn he was actually a murderer.

But at the same time, Nicky couldn't deny the evidence. The wallpaper. The lying about his identity. It was all pointing to him...

And so, they had to interrogate him.

"Mr. Dumond," Nicky said, "or should I say... Richard Fanson."

He looked up at her, shock in his bulging eyes. "No... I haven't heard that name in so long..."

"It's your real name," Ken said. "Your name is Richard Fanson from Brooklyn, New York."

"No... I'm Charles Dumond from Pine Grove... I've lived here my whole life..."

Nicky's heart twisted. Did he really believe that? Was he really so delusional that he thought he'd lived in this little town his entire life? Or was this all just an elaborate ruse—a man using mental health to shield him from the danger of being caught?

They were going to have to be careful with this one. They couldn't interrogate him or accuse him like they could any other perp. They needed to be more tactful, because he did, on file, have a diagnosed illness. Whether he was lying about it now to cover up would come to light, but Nicky had to handle him with care until then.

So, Nicky started with something lighter. She took out photos of the two victims, Paris and Francine. The third had not been ID'd yet. These were pictures of the girls, alive and well. She slid them across the table to Mr. Dumond.

"Do you know these girls, Mr. Dumond?" Nicky asked.

"No... I've never seen them before."

"Are you sure?" Ken asked, leaning forward. "Look very closely. You don't recognize them at all?"

He was baffled. "No! What is this about? Why did you take me from my shop?"

"You don't remember pointing a musket at us?" Nicky asked.

"What? Of course not!" he exclaimed.

The musket ended up being unloaded, but the fact remained. In his stupor, Mr. Dumond had resorted to violence, and that did not bode well for his innocence in this case.

"You said you were running from someone," Nicky said. "You thought we were some other people who were after you."

"That doesn't make any sense," Dumond said.

"What happened in New York?" Nicky asked.

Mr. Dumond's fingers curled into fists. "I can't--"

"Did you hurt those girls?" Ken asked.

"I... I..." Mr. Dumond whispered. "I can't remember..."

Nicky glanced at Ken. He nodded, and she took out the photo of Paris. "Is this the girl you can't remember?"

"No! I've never seen her!"

"Do you remember who you were before?" Nicky asked. "You lived in New York. You had a life there."

"No... no, this is my home. I'm Charles Dumond from Pine Grove. No one else. I don't know what you're talking about."

Nicky sighed. They needed to do this now. They needed to get to the bottom of this. "Mr. Dumond, we're not here to judge you. But if you killed those girls, we need you to come clean. We can't help you unless you're honest with us."

Mr. Dumond looked up at her. "I don't know what you're talking about..."

"Please, Mr. Dumond," Nicky said. "I know it's hard. But you have to trust us. We're not here to hurt you. We just need the truth. What happened in New York?"

Mr. Dumond's eyes flicked to hers. He looked terrified. "I... I..."

"It's okay, Mr. Dumond," Nicky said. "Tell us the truth. You won't be in trouble. We're here to help you." She hoped it would work, that the gentle approach would get through to him—being hostile in this situation would only freak him out, she was sure of that.

"You don't understand," Mr. Dumond whispered. "I can't remember."

"What do you mean?" Ken asked. “Can’t remember what?”

"I can't remember," he said. "I don't know who I am. I don't remember anything from before I came to Pine Grove."

"You mean, you can't remember anything in New York?" Nicky asked.

"No." Mr. Dumond's eyes were haunted. "It's all a blur. I have nightmares... I see things... I don't understand a lot of things... but I know I've never hurt any girls... not ever..."

Nicky sighed. Maybe there was no point to this. Clearly, Dumond was unwell. And Nicky wasn't sure talking in circles around him or trying to get him to remember things he clearly couldn't, would help. Nicky was trained in psychology and behavioral analysis, but first and foremost, her job was to catch killers. If they could get an actual psychologist in there, an expert on schizophrenia, maybe they could get Dumond to open up. They needed someone with a gentle, professional approach, someone who could actually help him in the long run, too.

Nicky stood up, and Ken did too. "Hey, where are you--"

"I need to talk to you," Nicky said. "Mr. Dumond, we'll be right back."

Nicky and Ken went into the hall. Once they were alone, Ken shot Nicky a stern look.

"What's going on? We barely even started," he said.

Nicky leaned against the wall. "I just don't know how much good this is doing us. Maybe we should call in a mental health professional."

"What, you actually believe his act?" Ken asked. "He could be making it all up, Lyons."

"I don't know," Nicky said. "But I do know that you have to have a heart in this job. And I can't do this to him anymore. He's so... vulnerable..."

"Are you serious?" Ken asked. "We have pictures of his victims! How is he vulnerable?"

"We don't know he took them," Nicky retorted, but she could feel Ken was getting heated. Clearly, his instincts were pushing him in a different direction. "I'm not saying we stop looking at him," Nicky said, "but we should just call in some extra help."

"That could take more time than we have," Ken said. "I say we keep questioning him until he gives us something useful."

"And what if he never does? What if he's innocent?" Nicky asked. "Ken, I know you're not a warm and fuzzy guy, but you can't just bully this poor man into confessing to something he didn't do."

"Don't go soft on me now, Lyons," Ken said. "We have a job to do. And we're going to do it. Don't get fooled by his whole 'confused old man' act. I'm not saying we need to bite his head off--maybe he is having some sort of mental break. But we need to keep on him."

For the first time in a while, Nicky felt the abrasive edge of Ken's words scrape at her. She was the one in charge of this task force--not him. Even if things had gotten romantic between them, she couldn't forget that.

"This is my task force," Nicky said, holding his gaze, "and if I say we need to bring someone else in to talk to him, then that's the route we're going to take."

Ken's eyes narrowed. "So that's how it is?" he said.

Nicky sighed. There was no way she was backing down. "Yeah, Ken. That's how it is."

"Fine," Ken said. "Find us a good psych then. I need to take five."

With that, Ken left, his shoes clacking against the floor as he made his way down the hall.

The whole situation seemed ridiculous to her. But there was no point in arguing. She needed to prove to herself that she wasn't softening up. That she was still tough. But that she also wasn't heartless.

***

"Agent Lyons, I'm Dr. Vale." A brunette woman with kind eyes held her hand out to Nicky, and Nicky shook it. They were in the lobby of the police station, and it was late now, but a few officers were still milling about.

"Thank you for coming in to help us so late," Nicky said. "Normally, the FBI has people for this, but we couldn't find anyone to come in on such short notice, and so quickly."

Dr. Helga Vale was a psychiatrist at the hospital here in Pine Grove, and Nicky had looked her up to see she was highly accredited. To Nicky's luck, she was able to make it in.

"Of course, I'm happy to help," Dr. Vale said, and the two of them made their way down the hall, toward the interrogation room.

"So, we have a schizophrenic male, seventy-one," Nicky explained. "We have circumstantial evidence that might link him to a series of murders, but with the mental state he seems to be in, we're not sure the best way to interrogate him. His real name is Richard Fanson from Brooklyn, New York, but he insists he's Charles Dumond from Pine Grove and has lived here his whole life."

"So, he's claiming retrograde amnesia?" Dr. Vale asked.

"Yes," Nicky said. "But he's also claiming to be innocent of these murders."

"I see," Dr. Vale said. "Well, that is certainly unusual. But I've dealt with many patients with his condition before. I might be able to talk to him. First, I want to make sure we're clear on your expectations. My understanding is that you want him to confess to murder."

"Yes," Nicky said. "But we're also here to help him. We're not trying to take advantage of his mental state. If he's innocent, or if he's suffering from a mental illness, we need to get him the help he needs."

"I understand," Dr. Vale said. "In that case, I should talk to him alone first and see what I can learn."

They reached the interrogation room door, where an officer was standing by. Nicky nodded at him.

"This officer here will be watching the whole time," Nicky said. "Mr. Dumond is restrained, so he can't harm you."

"Thank you, Agent Lyons." With that, Dr. Vale went into the room with the officer.

Nicky sighed, just as she realized Ken was standing at the end of the hall. Things felt tense between them now--like they were suddenly not on the same team.

"Hey," she said, walking up to him. "Have you eaten anything?"

"I'm fine," Ken said, but he was avoiding eye contact.

"Well... the doctor is in there, talking to him," Nicky said. "I think that's the best course of action."

"I know," Ken said, finally looking at her. "I know that. I'm sorry. I... I don't know. I guess I just have a lot on my mind."

"I get it, I do," Nicky said. "But if we're going to solve this case, we have to be on the same page. We can't let our personal dramas get in the way."

Ken sighed. "You're right," he said. "I'm sorry. I'm just... frustrated. I don't even know where to start. We've been having such a hard time getting a lead on this guy, and the guy in there is no help. I just... I hate feeling so helpless."

Nicky put a hand on his shoulder. She should have known he would take it badly. He was so headstrong, and so used to having the answers, that it must have been driving him crazy.

"It's okay," Nicky said. "We're going to get him. I promise. And we're going to do it together."

"Thanks," Ken said. "I appreciate that."

He leaned in, and for a moment, Nicky thought he was going to kiss her. But instead, he simply rested his forehead against hers, and she felt his hand come up and rest on the small of her back.

"I really do appreciate it," he said.

"We'll solve this," Nicky said, "and then we'll finally be able to relax together. How does that sound?"

"That sounds like a good plan," Ken said, and he pulled her in for a hug. When they pulled away, she let her hand slide down his arm and entwined her fingers with his. She felt a sense of relief that they had gotten past this little trouble.

Just then, Nicky's phone buzzed in her pocket. She let go of Ken's hand and pulled it out.

It was Chief Franco.

Nicky swallowed hard. "It's the chief."

"Shit, that might not be good," Ken said.

True. Oftentimes, when the chief called during a case, it was to deliver bad news.

With bated breath, Nicky answered the phone. "This is Agent Lyons."

"Lyons, it's Franco," he said. He sounded tired. "I assume you're with Walker now."

"Yeah..." Her eyes locked on Ken's. "We're together."

"Good. Because you two have somewhere to be." The chief took a breath. "They found a body."

CHAPTER SIXTEEN

The night sky was coated in inky clouds when Nicky pulled her car up to the crime scene, her heart in her throat, Ken quiet in the passenger seat. Through the windshield, police lights lit up the night, and caution tape barred off the entire area of an antique store called Smithson's.

There were police officers swallowing the scene, taking photos and running forensics, but between their moving bodies, Nicky made out the distinct shape of a body splayed out on the steps toward the store.

Bile churned in her gut. She parked the car, a good distance from the scene.

"Jesus," Ken said. "This doesn't look good."

"No," Nicky said. "I think it's safe to say that this is not good."

She unsnapped her seatbelt and got out of the car, stepping into the muggy, humid night. They were on the outskirts of town. The trees loomed dark and foreboding against the night sky, their branches swaying in the wind as they seemed to reach out menacingly toward Nicky and Ken. The shop looked small and abandoned, almost forgotten by time, if not for the officers surveying the scene.

Ken was close behind her. Together, the two of them walked toward the store and the body.

A shiver ran through Nicky. This guy was so methodical, and yet his pattern—it was changing, which made him more wildly unpredictable. What would he do next? Nicky wasn't sure, at this point. He was getting more brazen, more public. She was starting to get the sinking feeling that they were never going to catch him. He was going to keep going and going, killing people, and they were just going to be running after him.

"Can I help you?" someone asked.

Nicky turned around. A tall man with a goatee and graying hair stood behind them, dressed in a cop uniform. His badge identified him as a chief of police.

"Yeah," Nicky said, holding up her badge. "Agent Lyons, FBI. This is my partner, Agent Walker."

"Chief Schmitt," the man said. "This is my jurisdiction. I'm glad you two could make it out so late."

"Of course," Nicky said. "Who found the body?"

"The witness is over there," he said, nodding to beside the building, where a car was parked. A man sat on the hood, talking to two officers. "The guy claims he was driving into town when he saw a woman lying on the steps. At first, he thought she was drunk and wanted to help her, but the moment he saw blood, he called us."

Nicky swallowed hard, looking over at the store. "Mind taking us to the body?"

"Of course."

Chief Schmitt led the way, and Nicky and Ken followed. The chief stepped through the caution tape and over to the body. As they got closer, Nicky made out the details and felt a pang of despair in her chest. The woman's throat was slit messily, and she was wearing a vintage-style red dress, her body draped over the steps like she'd been dumped there. But it bore an eerie resemblance to the Polaroid photos of the other victims.

This was definitely done by the same guy.

Nicky closed her eyes for a moment, trying to find her control. She could tell this murder was fresh, based on the color of the victim's skin and the blood. Which meant they were just a little too late.

"I'm sorry," Chief Schmitt said. "I can imagine that this is hard for you. You see this stuff all the time, right?"

Nicky opened her eyes. "I've seen worse," she said, but her voice was hoarse. She cleared her throat. "Have you identified the victim yet?"

"One of our officers ID'd her as Marie Cooper," he said. "She's one of his friends' daughters. A local. Nobody knew she was missing."

Nicky frowned. "Wait, nobody knew?"

"No--the father claimed he saw her earlier today, and figured she was just out with friends. But the friends said they never saw her."

Nicky's heart raced--because for the first time, they had a concrete idea as to how long he might keep victims. They never found Paris, Francine, or the third victim--the Jane Doe's--body. All they had were the photos, but those could have been taken at any time.

But this girl, Marie, went missing today. The man took her today, and all within the span of twenty-four hours had killed her.

That was an extremely rapid timeline.

Nicky looked at the scene again. Something was taped to the glass doors. Stepping over the scene, Nicky walked up to it.

It was a Polaroid photo of Marie's body, taped right there.

The killer's M.O.

But this was the first time he had ever left a body.

He was accelerating.

"I guess he's getting more confident," Ken said, coming to stand behind Nicky.

"Or he's just getting sloppy," Nicky said.

"Maybe," Ken replied. "But what would make him feel confident enough to leave this body instead of moving it?"

"That's exactly the question we need to answer," Nicky said. She looked at the chief. "We need footage from every traffic camera in town. We're looking specifically for a 1998 Hana Kuma without a license plate." Now that Mr. Dumond could be ruled out as a suspect, Nicky was sure the car detail was what they had to focus on.

"I'll get on it," Chief Schmitt said. "And I'll have some officers canvass the area for anyone who might have seen something. There are some tracks in the mud, but it's hard to tell."

"Thank you," Nicky said.

The chief nodded and walked over to the officers at the car. He talked to them for a bit, then one of them went back to his car.

A gust of wind blew through the air, rustling the trees and making the caution tape flap in the wind.

They needed to catch this guy. Based on this timeline, he would choose another victim for his sick photography game.

And he would do it soon.

***

Nicky walked into the motel room, her eyes scanning the dingy space. She saw threadbare carpets and cracked walls, signs of neglect and disrepair. Nicky's bag landed heavily on the bed, making the cheap mattress bounce slightly. Ken followed her into the room, his footsteps heavy on the creaky floorboards.

It was a small highway motel, but it was the closest spot--it would have to do. They needed a place to sit down with the information and find something to lead them to the killer, and they had to do it fast.

Nicky set her laptop up at the table. No word from the police about the car yet, but she hoped something would come in soon. Until then, they needed to review every detail they had so far.

The killer was methodical. He always left a Polaroid at the scene, showing his handiwork. But this time, he had left the body.

And it was the first time he had done that. Why now?

The killer was never careless, never left behind evidence that could be traced back to him. He was always careful, always careful to leave nothing.

Nicky knew that leaving the body was deliberate. But why would he do that? She thought about the other victims. They were all pretty, slim, and had dark hair. They all looked like they could be related. That had to be a clue, but it was too broad of a hint to narrow down. Maybe there was a girl like that in the killer's life, a mother, sister, lover, who he was obsessed with, but she couldn't just look at men with an affiliation to every brunette woman in the country. That would put Nicky on the list too.

No, they needed something else.

As Ken sat with her at the table, Nicky splayed the four photos of the victims out. One was on the floor. The other in a chair. Two were on couches.

"Could there be something in their poses?" Nicky asked absently.

"What?" Ken asked.

"The killer takes the photos to get a thrill, but they are ritualistic too. He takes one of the girls in a different pose every time." She tapped the photos. "He likes to act out a fantasy with every victim, but there has to be more to it than that. He must have a reason to select a certain position."

Nicky leaned back in her chair, tapping her fingers on the armrest. What could he be trying to get out of it? She looked down at the photos again. What was the significance of the framing?

"What if he's trying to tell us something?" Ken said.

Nicky looked up. "What do you mean?"

"What if he's trying to communicate something to us?" Ken said. He leaned in, his eyes shining. "What if this is his way of showing us that he's in complete control of these girls?"

"That would make sense," Nicky said. She picked up the photos. "He is showing us that he's in control, and he can do whatever he wants with them."

"And he takes these photos to assert his dominance," Ken said. "He wants to show us that the girls are helpless, that they are completely at his mercy."

Nicky's eyes scanned the photos again. She could see it now. The girls were posed in ways that made them look more like objects than people.

"These girls were taken right out of their normal lives," Ken said. "Every time he takes a girl, he's stealing her away from her family, her friends, her job. He's taking her from everything she knows, and into this completely foreign world."

"You're saying he's trying to show us how powerless his victims are?" Nicky said.

Ken nodded. "It would make sense. He's trying to prove to us that he has absolute, complete control over these girls. If he can just take them away from everything they know and force them to do whatever he wants, then he's proving that he's in complete control of their lives."

Nicky leaned back in her chair, looking at the photos again. The killer took his photos with care, framing them perfectly. He wanted them to look good.

But was there more to it than that?

She wasn't sure. What she did know was that her mind wasn't feeling like it was in the right place. She needed something, something to get her thinking on the right track. The thought of losing another girl frustrated her to no end.

Nicky stood up, feeling uncomfortable in her own skin. "I'm gonna take a walk."

With that, she left the hotel room.

CHAPTER SEVENTEEN

The sky had cleared, revealing a brilliant moon, as Nicky crossed the motel parking lot, her hands in her pockets. She needed to clear her head, empty all of these thoughts, but she wasn't sure how.

There were too many things happening in her mind. It was like she was in overdrive, and her CPU was about to burn out. Worries about the case, about not finding the killer, the lack of clues, and, of course, Rosie. Always lurking in her mind, distracting her sometimes.

Nicky sighed as she walked aimlessly. If she could clear her head, maybe she could get a blank slate to work off. But it seemed like an impossible task.

Nicky was so lost in thought that she didn't pay attention to where she was going. Her mind was just spinning with possibilities, ideas, and plans. Her feet carried her forward, walking her past the highway and into the woods.

Nicky looked up. The trees were tall and spindly, the branches making it seem like the stars were further away. Nicky could see the narrow road curving off, but there were no cars driving on it.

She was alone, and she needed a break.

A chill went down her spine, sending shivers up her arms. The woods were quiet tonight, not a single noise from a bird or an animal. It was dark, oppressive, and she never felt like she was safe within the trees, not after what had happened when she was younger.

Turning away from the trees, she made her way back over to the motel parking lot, no closer to clearing her mind.

Normally, in a time like this, Nicky would be able to call her psychiatrist, Dr. Graham. It had been a while since she'd seen him; she had been focusing on her cases, and her own healing, but giving little time to care for her own mental health. It was late, almost midnight, but she wondered if Dr. Graham might be around to talk. She took out her phone and tried his number.

"Hello," Dr. Graham said. He sounded tired.

"Dr. Graham, it's Nicky," Nicky said. "I know it's late, but I'm having trouble coping. I just need to talk."

"Nicky? I haven't heard from you in a while--you know I'm always here to take your calls. How are you holding up?"

Dr. Graham asked.

"Well, I guess I'm having a rough time of it," she said. "I'm working on a case that I just can't seem to get a handle on. I'm having trouble thinking straight about it."

"You need to step back from the case," Dr. Graham said. "Take a break, clear your mind."

"I know, I know, I've tried that, but when I close my eyes, all I see is another girl, another victim."

"I know it's hard, but you need to focus on your own self-care. You can't help anyone until you're able to help yourself," Dr. Graham said. "Don't get me wrong, I know you want to save these girls, but you can't do anything if you're not healthy yourself. There's nothing worse than helping someone when you're unstable."

"I know, I know. I'm just having a hard time with it," Nicky said. She was thankful to have Dr. Graham to talk to. He always understood her and her worries, and there was something about his voice that was soothing. "I'm just not sure what to do. I've tried everything."

"Well, I know you won't divulge much about your case to me, Nicky," he said. "But I know you. Sometimes, when you're not on the right track, it's because you've focused too much on one thing and missed details. Maybe the clue has been right in front of you all along, and you just need to look at it from another angle."

"I know what you're saying, but I feel like I've already tried that," Nicky said. "I'm open to suggestions, I just don't know what to do."

"Then try not to focus too much on one thing. Try to look at the big picture... who are you really hunting?"

Nicky stopped to think about it. Maybe Dr. Graham could help her sort out a profile of this guy.

"If I tell you a few things we know, do you think you can help me build a profile?" Nicky asked.

"Well, of course, I'd love to help if I can."

"Okay." She took a deep breath and paced, looking up at the night sky for a moment. "We have a man who takes vintage-style Polaroid photos of women he's killed and leaves them in antique stores for people to find. We've found three photos in antique stores, and more recently, he left a body outside of one with a photo as well."

"Wow," said Dr. Graham. "That's no small feat. But this can say a lot about him. It sounds like it's art to him... you might be dealing with a narcissist, maybe a failed photographer or artist who believed their work deserved more praise, and this is their way of forcing people to acknowledge and see them."

The moment Dr. Graham spoke, it clicked for Nicky. That made perfect sense.

"It's sad, because that means he probably has low self-esteem, and he might be socially awkward, maybe even shy," Nicky said.

"Well, that's the thing about narcissists. That's why they feel the need to be better than everyone else. It could be that he feels the need to be on top, better than everyone else, to be worthy of anything," Dr. Graham said. "It's sad that he feels that way, but it's also a weakness. It means you can use it against him. But Nicky, don't start to empathize with him too much. This is a person with no conscience, based on what you've described to me."

"I know," Nicky said. She was silent for a few moments more, and Dr. Graham remained quiet and calm. He knew that she needed time to think.

"He's been killing for a while, because he's smart," Nicky said. "He doesn't leave any evidence behind, and he's careful about everything he does. He's a perfectionist, and he must be very organized. He's had to plan this for a long time before he started, because he's smart enough to know that he's leaving a lot of evidence that could be found, even evidence he can't control." Nicky bit her lip. "I don't really know what to think of this guy. It's like he thinks he's a movie star, or something, doing these murders to get attention."

"Yeah, that could be. It's strange... but it's not strange if he's a narcissist. They will do anything to make sure they're seen. In this case, it's probably because he's not getting the attention he needs. Being a murderer isn't strange in the slightest to him. He's probably done it to others in the past, as well."

"You know, you're probably right about that," Nicky said. "I'm going to have to look back at the other cases... but I'm also going to have to figure out where he'd go from here. I mean, he's already done all this, so what's the next step for him? How does he get his victims?"

"Well, narcissists usually don't like to follow the rules of society. They feel like the rules don't apply to them because they're so special," Dr. Graham said. "So it might be that he chooses a conventional way to meet victims, like in a bar or at an event or the grocery store. If he thinks he's so good that he won't get caught, he's probably bold enough to go in public."

"Yeah, that makes sense," Nicky said.

"It's sad that he has low self-esteem, but it's good to know how he thinks. It can help you catch him," Dr. Graham said. "But Nicky, the most important thing, is that you have to take care of yourself. You have to focus on your own mental health. If you don't, you're useless to all these girls. You can't help if you're not capable of helping yourself first."

"I know. I know," Nicky said. "I'm just sorry that I've been so bad at it."

"Well, that's why you have me," Dr. Graham said. "And you can always come back to me. I'm always here for you."

"Thanks, Dr. Graham." Nicky smiled, feeling warm inside. "It was good talking again. I promise I've made progress in other aspects of my life, and I'll come see you in person soon to talk it out."

"I look forward to it. Good luck, Nicky."

With that, the call ended. But Nicky was feeling more confident and motivated now. The idea that this guy was a narcissistic artist leaving his mark on these antique stores seemed to be the right track. And Nicky realized that she'd been focusing so much on the details of the poses, and the equipment the killer used, that she did let one crucial detail slip by her: the actual stores in which they were found.

Yes, they were all antique shops. But what if it was more than that? Each photo was found at a different antique store, which showed them that the killer, most likely, was a fan of antiques. Harriet's Antiques. Olden's Antiques. And at last, Smithson's. Harriet, Olden, Smithson.

Nicky paused, the gears in her mind turning. A thought came to her: *What if the names of the stores are a clue?*

This could be it. She rushed into the motel room to tell Ken.

CHAPTER EIGHTEEN

"The names?" Ken asked, lifting a brow. "How do you figure?"

Nicky sat across from him in the motel room. She hadn't fully figured it out yet--but something told her this was the ticket.

"Well, first, there was Harriet's Antiques. Then Olden's. Then Smithson's," Nicky said. "It could be a longshot, but maybe there's some sort of code in the names."

"Maybe," Ken said, "but what makes you think that?"

"Because this guy wants to be known," Nicky said. "He's not doing this for fun. It's more personal to him. He wants to leave his personal mark, and I don't believe he hasn't put his name on this thing. If we look closer, we might find something."

Ken nodded. "I see where you're going. Let's see what we can find."

Nicky sat up a little taller in her chair. "This could be it. I'm sure of it."

"Okay, then," Ken said. "Let's look closer. The first store was Harriet's."

"Harriet," Nicky said, thinking. "Harriet. Harriet..." She scribbled the name down on a sheet of paper.

"Alright, the next store was Olden's," Ken said. "Olden. Olden... Olden... "

"Olden," Nicky said. "Olden... Olden..."

When she wrote it down, she noticed something interesting. Harriet was a woman's name, and Nicky felt sure they weren't looking for a woman in this case. It was possible, but she doubted it, especially with the footage of the man with the car.

But could it be part of the name?

She squinted. "Could it be... Harold?"

"Harold?" Ken lifted brow.

"Harriet and Olden. Combine them, you get the first name 'Harold.'"

Ken nodded, understanding filling his eyes. "Then the last name could be Smithson? Or just Smith?"

"Harold Smith," Nicky said aloud. "If we narrow down any Harold Smith or Smithsons in Florida with a 1998 Hana Kuma, then we might be onto something."

Maybe it was a longshot. Maybe this whole idea was off the mark, but based on this guy's profile, it seemed completely possible he'd leave a mark like that.

"That's a good start," Ken said. "You're right. He's narcissistic, but he's also very careful. He isn't an idiot."

"Right," Nicky said, nodding. "He knows what he's doing, which means he's using his name."

"Right. But it's still a lot of work. We'll have to go through every Harold Smith or Smithson with a Hana vehicle registered in 1998. It's going to take a while."

Nicky grabbed her laptop and opened it up. "Not if we narrow down the list," she said. "We're looking for a man named Harold Smith or Smithson, with a Hana Kuma, between the ages of twenty and fifty. Likely with a criminal record. Let's start there. We can do this."

"Okay, you narrow down the list," Ken said. "I'll make some calls."

Nicky began to type. "Thanks, Ken. This means a lot to me," she said.

"You mean a lot to me. We're in this together," Ken said, putting a hand on Nicky's shoulder.

She smiled, feeling herself blush. She cleared her throat and got back to work.

There were many people with the name Harold Smith or Harold Smithson in Florida. However, only fifteen of them were registered to have a Hana Kuma car--and only three of those happened to have the 1998 model.

Harold Smith from Miami. Sixty-one years old, a bit older than their profile, but still possible. He had no criminal record, but had been reported for sexual harassment once in his fifties. Miami was also where Paris Conner went missing, so it was possible, although it seemed he still resided there, which made his guilt less likely. They were looking for someone in the area nearby, judging by the way the killer had taken the photos in a basement then dropped the fresh body.

Harold Smithson from Jacksonville. It was only about an hour and a half away, very possible to have traveled here in that time. He was a school teacher, forty-one years old, and had been arrested for theft in his twenties. It seemed he turned his life around. A fair suspect, Nicky thought, but not exactly the top pick.

No, her top pick was Harold Smith from Green Valley--which happened to be only twenty minutes away from where they were now.

This Harold Smith did not have a job. He was married with a child, thirty-eight years old, and he had a criminal record. Nicky wondered if his wife knew that in his early twenties, he had been charged with sexual battery in relation to an incident that occurred inside a frat house he was part of. Charges were pressed against him and two other boys--a truly sick crime. But his record had been clean since then.

Nicky looked at his mugshot from back then--a stone-faced man with no remorse in his eyes, and a flaccid smile. A more recent photo of him showed a similar face, only with more lines.

He gave Nicky the creeps.

Ken came back over, hanging up his phone call. "Still no hits on the car in town," he said.

"But I'm gonna call Grace and--"

"Don't worry about that," Nicky cut in. "I think I have our suspects."

Ken's brows went up. "What do you mean?"

"I narrowed it down to these three Harolds," Nicky said. "They're the only ones with a 1998 Hana Kuma. One is thirty-eight, one is forty-one, and one is sixty-one. I don't think our killer is sixty-one, but that leaves the other two."

"Okay," Ken said. "So, you narrowed it down to those two. So, what do you think? Are they the killers?"

"I think it's possible," Nicky said. "But, I mean, it's not exactly concrete. One guy lives just twenty minutes from here. I think he's our top pick."

Ken nodded, obviously agreeing with her. "You're right," he said, "but we should send officers to talk to the other two as well."

Excitement moved through Nicky. This was finally something they could work on. "Agreed. Let's give them a call and visit Harold Smith from Green Valley ourselves." She stood and grabbed her keys. "Come on. I'll drive."

They rushed out of the motel, a determined energy between them, and got into Nicky's car. As Nicky started it up, Ken called about the other two Harolds. Nicky could hear the officer on the other end agree to send people to look into both suspects, just to be safe--but Nicky had a feeling the one they were looking for, they were about to come eye-to-eye with.

She belted down the dark back-road highway, the night sky clear above.

She could see stars glittering like jewels above her. The lights of oncoming traffic flashed upon her face and trees rustled. She drove in silence, the seatbelt holding her tight, the windows shut tight to keep out the world. In that moment, everything in her life felt purposeful--she was here, with Ken, on their way to make what she hoped would be a successful arrest.

She hoped she could save whoever he had his eye on next.

Until then, they were on the open road. As they drove, Nicky couldn't help but imagine what this man's victims went through. She imagined the fear, the feeling of the unknown, because it was exactly what Nicky had felt when she'd been kidnapped all those years ago. The difference was, these girls were killed, and Nicky had been able to get away.

Rosie slinked back into her mind. Her sister, who never got away either.

Nicky's stomach twisted as she imagined a possibility in which, maybe, she was too late to save Rosie too. Rosie's body had never been found, but that didn't mean there wasn't one.

Still... Nicky had to hold onto hope. She had to believe her sister was alive out there.

She had to hope that she would be able to give her sister justice.

Nicky gripped the steering wheel tighter and focused on the road. She thought about her sister, and how she was going to find her.

She glanced at Ken, who was looking out the window, lost in thought. Ever since she'd met Ken, she'd felt a bond with him, but now she felt something that went beyond that.

She wondered if he felt it too, if he felt the energy between them the same way she did. It was more than feelings, more than liking each other... she felt connected to him, like he was in this with her.

He turned to look at her. Their eyes met, and she felt a moment of pause.

The air between them seemed to get thicker and she felt her heart beating faster. It was as if they were a static charge, attracted to each other. She pushed her feelings aside and turned to face the road, remembering that earlier, they'd had a bit of a tiff over how to handle Charles Dumond. Ken had gotten snappy with her, and in turn, Nicky had to activate the side of her that was in charge. They hadn't talked about Charles yet.

"Hey, Ken," Nicky said. "Are you still upset about the Dumond thing earlier?"

"What?" Ken said. "No... you were right, Lyons, he wasn't our guy."

"Yeah, but I..." She bit her lip. This wasn't easy. "I know I got a little stern with you."

He laughed once. "You mean when you said 'this is my task force.'"

"Yeah," she said. "I mean, it is."

"I know it is." He sighed. "No hard feelings. I get it. I wanted to do something else, but in the end, you call the shots. It was professional, not personal. I get it, Lyons." He turned away with a grin. "Besides, it's kind of hot when you put me in my place."

Nicky felt her cheeks flush, and all she could do was laugh. "If you say so, Walker."

She turned back to the road, but relief flowed through her. Things were going to work out. Mr. Dumond was getting the care he needed, and this Harold Smith guy--he was going to get caught.

Nicky would make sure of it.

CHAPTER NINETEEN

A few minutes later, Nicky pulled up to the curb in front of a small, two-story house in Green Valley. It was a quaint neighborhood with small houses nestled cozily in the rolling green hills. The soft glow of street lamps illuminated the trees and houses, casting a warm yellow light over everything, and creating a country feel. Nicky could see a driveway, which wound around to the back of the house, and there, was a Hana Kuma.

"Looks like we've found our guy," Nicky said, her heart racing. But she'd been in situations like this before. They had to expect the worst--when caught, this guy could totally flip his switch... he might even be armed.

"I'm ready," Ken said. "Hopefully he doesn't mind being taken down this late."

Nicky stepped out of her car and Ken followed. They approached the house, and as they did, Nicky noticed a dimness to the lights inside. It was as if the lights were off, but some were on in the very corners of the rooms.

"Strange," Ken said.

"Yeah," Nicky said. "But it's after midnight. Maybe Mr. Smith went to bed."

They went up to the door and knocked loudly. Nothing. Again, and there was a noise somewhere in the housc--thc sound of an infant crying. Nicky had read in his file that he had a kid, a baby, and for a moment, she hoped that maybe she was wrong about this.

But then she remembered the mugshot... and the sexual battery charge in his twenties... no, this wasn't a man with a completely innocent past, even if he did have a life and a family now.

The baby's cries stopped. After a moment, a man wearing a white tee and plaid pajamas answered. He had an eerily calm expression--just like the mugshot--but he was a very normal-looking man. Average height, brown hair and eyes, Caucasian. At first glance, one wouldn't guess anything was off about him at all.

But Nicky saw something in his eyes--something empty.

"Excuse me?" he said. "It's very late--"

"Mr. Harold Smith?" Nicky asked.

"Yes?" the man said. "Can I help you?"

"We're here to ask you a few questions." Nicky flashed her badge, along with Ken. "I'm Agent Nicky Lyons. This is my partner, Agent Ken Walker. We're sorry to bother you so late."

A calm smile spread on his lips. "Oh... that is okay. It's a good thing we called the nanny in tonight to help with JJ... my wife is at work."

"Does your wife often work nights?" Ken asked.

"She does," said Harold. "She's a nurse. Oncology. Quite the spectacular woman. But I stay at home to take care of our son. Sometimes I need a little help, though."

"So, your nanny is inside," Nicky clarified.

"Yes," Harold said. "She's in the den. Do you need to speak with her?"

"When she's available, that would be great," Nicky said.

He opened the door wider. "Well, please, come in."

Nicky nodded to Ken, and they stepped inside.

Harold's house was warm, cozy, and tastefully decorated. It was also immaculate. It was like a show home. The floors were spotless, and the walls were covered in framed family photos.

"My wife is a bit of a neat freak," Harold said. "She loves taking care of things. It's her calling."

"What about you?" Nicky asked.

"Me?" Harold said. "I don't think I have a calling. I just do whatever I'm needed to do." He smiled. "It's a good thing I'm needed at home."

"Yeah," Nicky said. "You're a family man."

"Yes," Harold said.

"Do you know why we're here?" Ken asked.

"No idea," said Harold. "I barely even leave the house anymore."

"What do you do at home?" Ken asked.

"Take care of JJ, make arts and crafts... what else can a stay-at-home dad do? It's a bit of a dream come true, if I'm being honest."

"Do you have any hobbies?" Ken asked.

"I don't have time for hobbies," Harold said, with a laugh. "But I do love to draw and paint, and I do quite a bit of sewing during my free time."

"Sewing?" Ken said.

"Yes," Harold said. "It's not very manly, but I enjoy it."

"I don't see anything wrong with that," Nicky said.

Harold smiled. "Not many people do."

Nicky looked around the house. It was such a quaint family home. If Harold was trying to seem normal, he was doing a damn good job of it. But still... Nicky couldn't shake that something was off with him. He was calm. Too calm.

"Do you mind if I have a moment alone with your nanny?" Nicky asked.

If the nanny came often to take care of the son while the wife was at work, then she would know if Harold left the house--giving him time to commit the murders.

Harold shrugged. "Sure. I'll go grab her and JJ."

"Thank you," Nicky said.

Harold disappeared back down the hallway and, this time, Nicky heard a door shut.

"You think he's the guy?" Ken whispered.

"I think his reaction was a little... off," Nicky whispered back. "He didn't seem at all curious or worried that we were here."

"Well, he's pretty damn nice," Ken said. "I mean, he's either the nicest guy I've ever met, or one of the best actors ever."

Nicky looked down the dark hall. She was thinking it was the latter.

Moments later, Harold emerged with an elderly woman with white hair and glasses. The woman hobbled toward the living room.

"Good evening, ma'am," Nicky said.

"Evening?" The old woman chuckled. "It's a little past that, my dear. I'm Margaret. Mr. Smith says you'd like a word with me? I can talk now, while the baby is sleeping."

"Thank you." Nicky shot Ken a look, and he nodded. Nicky left him alone with Harold in the living room, then followed Margaret into the kitchen. The kitchen was spotless, with gleaming stainless-steel appliances and sparkling countertops. Bright, moonlight-filled windows offered a view of a lush garden full of flowers and herbs. Pots of vibrant green plants hung on the walls or stood on shelves, lending a cheerful feel to the room.

Margaret adjusted her glasses as they faced each other. "Mr. Smith said you're with the FBI? What's this all about?"

"We're just covering all our bases, ma'am," Nicky said. "Nothing to be alarmed about. I did want to ask you a few questions about Mr. Smith."

"Well, okay." Margaret wrung her pale hands together.

"How long have you been working for him?"

"Only a few months now, since JJ was born," she said. "It's hard for the poor family to deal with the baby all alone sometimes. Mrs. Smith brings all the money home, but Mr. Smith has trouble sleeping, so I'm here to take the edge off a little."

"I'm sure it's been very helpful," Nicky said.

"It has," Margaret said. "I'm not very good in the kitchen, but Mr. Smith is. He makes the best meals I've ever had in my life, and we're all quite thankful for that. I'm sure you can imagine: a baby is a whole lot of work."

"I'm sure," Nicky said. "You stay here during the nights, then?"

"I do," Margaret said. "The wife goes to work around eight and comes back in the very early morning. I stay here until she comes to relieve me. It's been a lifesaver for the family."

"I see. And during the times you are here, do you ever see Mr. Smith leave the house?"

Margaret looked around for a moment, almost guiltily. She went quiet, then asked, "Is Mr. Smith in trouble?"

"Like I said," Nicky replied, "we're just covering our bases and ruling people out."

"Well, what's it about?"

"I can't classify that at this time." Nicky's patience was running thin. She understood Margaret was probably trying to be a good person, but this was life or death for the girls. "Please, Margaret, it's important that you tell us if Mr. Smith sometimes goes out at night, for any period of time at all."

"Well... yes, sometimes he does," Margaret said. "I do believe he is meeting with friends at a bar."

Nicky took out her notepad and pen from her jacket pocket. "And what are his friends' names?"

"I believe there's Dave Applegate, then Greg French. They're young dads too."

"And what about earlier tonight?" Nicky asked. "Were you left alone with the baby at all tonight?"

"Hmm, I think he did go out for a few drinks earlier, yes."

Nicky's heart raced. "About what time?"

"Maybe ten or so? He is normally only gone for a couple of hours."

All at once, Nicky's mouth went dry--and this suddenly felt very real. The timeline matched up. Harold Smith could have left his house, gone and taken the woman's body, and dropped it off at the store. He was in the area. He wasn't home at the time.

He had the car.

The name.

It was all adding up.

"Thank you, Margaret," Nicky said, as she stood. "You've been a huge help."

"Is Mr. Smith in trouble?" Margaret asked.

"I just told you," Nicky said. "I can't classify that at this time."

Margaret waved her hand. "I understand. But please--be careful with that man. He's a sweetheart."

Nicky nodded, and she left the kitchen.

Harold was sitting on a couch, looking as innocent as could be. Ken was standing in the corner, his posture tense.

Relief flooded through Nicky. The evidence was there, right in front of her. She wanted to scream. She wanted to lunge at Harold and lock him up right then and there.

But she stayed calm. She had to. She needed to get information, needed to make sure that what she was doing was the right thing. Sometimes what seemed like evidence was wrong, Nicky knew that, and she had to rely on facts and facts alone, not just feelings of certainty.

"Everything okay?" Harold asked.

"Just talking with Margaret," Nicky replied. "Actually, Mr. Smith, would you mind coming with us to the local police station? We'd like to ask you some more questions there."

Calmly, Harold rose. This was usually the time when a suspect would start to sweat or run away--but that didn't happen.

"Sure, I'd be happy to help," Harold said. "I'm not sure what this is about, but it seems very important."

He was… cooperating? In Nicky's experience, that was rare. Perps loved to run off and cause trouble for her.

"It is, sir," Nicky said. "We're just trying to rule people out."

"Well, I hope it's not one of my neighbors. I'd hate to think of anyone I know being involved in something like this."

"Me too," Nicky said.

Nicky nodded, and then she exchanged a long look with Ken.

They had him. Or at least, he might be the one they were looking for.

And now, all that was left to do was close the case.

CHAPTER TWENTY

The local police station was small and cramped, and most of the officers were yawning their way through the night--but Nicky was able to secure a small interrogation room for them to question Harold Smith in.

Now, Nicky sat opposite him with Ken at her side, and Harold still wore that calm, eerie smile, like he was unbothered by all of this. Certainly not the deranged type Nicky was used to dealing with, but maybe he was very good at closing off his emotions. Who knew what was really behind that calm smile?

"I'm sure you've realized by now that this is a bit more than a casual questioning," Nicky said. Now that they had him, the need for pleasantries were over--but she had to admit, it was nice to bring a perp in willingly for once, rather than having him try to kill her.

Before they'd come in, though, Nicky and Ken had called the two "friends" who Harold allegedly had been going out for drinks with. And those men confirmed that Harold was not with them tonight--nor had he been with them for months. They said he just had a baby and had dropped off the map, which didn't line up with Margaret's story at all.

Harold had been lying to Margaret. So where had he really been going?

To wherever he was keeping the girls he killed?

Harold only smiled. "It does look that way, Agent Lyons. Might I ask what you think I've done?"

Nicky opened up the file in front of them. She pulled out copies of the four photos, then slid them across to Harold. He looked down at them, but still, no hint of emotion crossed his brow.

"Those are quite graphic," he said. "You think I did this?"

"We're look for a man around your age, Harold, with a 1998 Hana Kuma. We believe the person driving that car has murdered and photographed these women, leaving them in antique stores around the area."

"And I'm a suspect," Harold said matter-of-factly. "I can't imagine what I've done to get on that list. I do have the car, but..."

"But what?"

"But I would never kill anyone," Harold said. "You don't seem to understand me. I'm a good person, Agent Lyons. I'm involved in the community, I volunteer at the local school, I help my family as much as I can. I am kind, generous, and gentle. I would never kill someone."

"Has that always been the case, though, Harold?" Nicky asked, and for the first time, something flashed in Harold's eyes. "We know about the sexual battery charge. We know what happened in your twenties."

Harold averted his eyes. "That... was a complicated situation."

Ken laughed once. "What the fuck is complicated about sexual battery? You were charged with it, bud, so drop the nice guy act."

"I'm not acting," Harold said. "I was with two boys at a fraternity when I was younger, yes. They did assault a girl, and I did nothing to stop it--but I didn't partake it in myself. Not at all. In fact, I was sleeping at the time. The girl lumped me in with the friends, though. Maybe she thought I was awake and just chose not to do anything, I don't know. But I never assaulted anyone."

"Not even a little?" Ken asked.

"No, not at all," Harold said. "I don't know what my past does to your case, but it has nothing to do with this crime."

"It tells us that you're willing to look the other way," Nicky said. "You're willing to let people do cruel things, and that's not the kind of person we want to have walking around. What would you do if you saw a friend hurting a woman? Would you help her?"

"Of course, I would," Harold replied.

"Then why didn't you do anything when you were in college?"

Harold didn't answer, and Ken leaned in. "What were you doing back then, Harold?"

"I was trying to get some sleep," Harold said. "I was tired, and I wanted to leave the next day, so I went to bed. I didn't know what was going on."

"You were a bystander," Nicky said.

"I was not a bystander. I was an unknowing participant."

"You were there when the girl was assaulted," Ken said. "You could have stopped it."

"I already explained that to you," Harold said. "I was tired. I didn't know what was going on."

"A jury didn't seem to think that," Nicky said.

"A jury is allowed to make mistakes," Harold said smoothly. "I guess that girl was upset about the boys. It happens. I don't blame her for lashing out."

"But even so," Ken said. "You didn't stop it. You walked away from a rape, and then you let your friends get away with it. You're one hell of a good guy, aren't you?"

Harold's face was stone. "I have made mistakes, Agent. I won't deny that. I was young and foolish, and I made mistakes. But I can tell you, I've grown up since then. I've changed. I'm a different person now."

"You're right," Nicky said. "You are a different person. You're not a nice guy. You're a predator, Harold. You prey on innocent women, and you kill them. You took those women and you photographed them and left the pictures in antique stores you frequent."

"I don't understand why you're looking for me," Harold said. "It's definitely not me in those photos."

"You're on the shortlist of suspects," Ken said. "We have your car; we have your name. We have good reason to think you're our guy."

"I understand." Harold nodded. "But naturally, I did not kill anyone. You're going to want proof that I am who I say I am. You want to talk to my wife and my family. You'll want to know where I was when this happened."

"We want to know where you were tonight, Harold," Nicky said.

Once more, Harold's eyes flashed. Something--almost like fear--flickered across his face.

Got him.

"Margaret said you went out tonight with your friends," Nicky said. "But we called them, and they haven't been out with you in months. So where have you been going while your wife is at work, Harold?"

Harold's eyes darted from side to side. For a moment, Nicky thought he might be about to bolt, but then he seemed to steady himself. "I go out alone. I told Margaret I was going with friends because it was easier to explain. I go to a bar called The Rusty Anchor."

"What do you do when you get there?" Nicky asked, even though she wasn't buying this at all.

"I sit, I talk to the owner," Harold said.

"You go specifically to this bar to talk to the owner?"

"Yeah," Harold said. "His name is Robert. I like talking to him."

"You go to a bar to talk to the owner," Ken said. "And you don't drink anything."

Harold's expression didn't change. "I don't drink. Not anymore. I used to, but I stopped about a year ago. I don't want to put poison in my body."

"You go out for drinks, and you don't drink," Ken said. "Then what do you do?"

"I leave," Harold said. "I come home."

"You just come home," Nicky said. "No hanging out, no talking to anyone. You come home, alone."

Harold nodded. "That's right."

"You know we can find this Robert, and he can tell us the truth," Nicky said.

"If he's even real," Ken added on.

Still, Harold's eyes were darting around. "I... well..."

"Where were you really going, Harold?" Nicky asked, leaning forward.

This was the part where he could come clean about it all. The murders. The photographs. He was backed into a corner...

But what Harold did next made Nicky's head spin. His character completely shifted. He dug his hands into his hair and pulled. "No... no..."

"Harold," Nicky said, wondering if he was about to snap. They didn't cuff him, as he didn't present any danger--but Nicky was wondering if that was now a mistake.

"No, they can't find out," Harold said.

"Find out what?" Ken pressed. "Tell us, you son of a bitch, or else--"

"There's someone else, okay?" Harold lifted his eyes, for the first time, showing real emotion: tears in his eyes. "I'm seeing another woman. I'm in love with someone other than my wife, and that's where I've been going. That's where I was tonight."

Silence filled the room. If this was another lie, Nicky was going to blow a fuse. For now, she had to play along.

"What's her name?" Nicky asked.

"I... I can't tell you her name," Harold said.

"Why not?"

"Because she's married," Harold said. "If her husband finds out, he'll kill me."

"She's married?" Nicky tried to keep her voice calm. "And you're seeing her anyway?"

"I can't help myself," Harold said. "I love her, and I want to be with her. I'm going to leave home--"

"Oh, you're going to leave your wife," Nicky said. "You're going to break up two marriages to be with her? What about your son, Harold?"

"I can't help it," Harold said. "I love her."

"You love her, so you're going to break up a marriage?" Nicky was getting tired of Harold's bullshit. "What is she, your soulmate or something?"

"Yes," Harold said, without missing a beat. "She's my soulmate. I've never met anyone like her, and I know I never will again. She's destiny." He shrugged. "I can't help it."

"Where does she live?" Nicky asked, fighting the urge to laugh at the absurdity of this.

"She's living with her husband," Harold said. "But I'll get her away from him. I've been working on it for a while."

"What's her name?" Nicky asked.

"I can't tell you her name," Harold said. "I'm sorry. I can't. It's too dangerous."

"If you don't tell us, we're going to book you for these murders," Nicky said, keeping her voice stern to show she wasn't messing around. "As far as I'm concerned, Harold, this is just another one of your lies--so unless you want to go to prison, you better tell us the name of this woman who can apparently prove your innocence."

"She's not joking, Harold," Ken added on. "Think about this. Think really hard."

Harold sniffled, before he pathetically nodded. "A-Adaline Jones," he managed. "She can vouch for me... I was with her... I never killed anyone..."

Nicky and Ken both scoffed. This guy was unbelievable.

"You're a real piece of work, Smith," Ken said. "We'll call this Adaline Jones girl and confirm your alibi. But I hope you know how much of a piece of shit you are for what you're doing to your family."

Nicky loathed the man in front of her now more than ever. As a child, she remembered her father would sometimes go out at night for hours to go drinking, and sometimes he'd come home at four in the morning and Nicky's late mother would be yelling at him. Sometimes, Nicky and Rosie would sit the top of the stairs and listen. They'd hear things about "other women." Nicky was sure her father was a serial cheater, and she hated the way it affected her mom.

Now, it was clear--this man, Harold Smith, was a serial cheater. He was a sociopath who was using his wife. He was using his wife's income to support his lavish habits and his new lover's lifestyle, and his wife was none the wiser.

"... I know," Harold said, dropping his hands into his lap. "I know."

"If you love her so much, why don't you just leave your wife?" Nicky asked.

"Because of my son," Harold said. "I don't want to break up my family."

"Wow," Ken muttered, shaking his head. "A real prince."

"I don't want any more lies," Nicky said. "This is your alibi. Adaline Jones. You love her, and you want to leave your wife for her. That's it, right?"

Harold didn't answer. He just looked down at his hands.

"Harold?" Nicky asked. "Harold, look at me."

He didn't look up. He just kept staring at his lap.

"Harold?" Ken asked. "Hey, Harold, if this is another lie, you're going to get arrested and go to prison. Four people are dead. Four people. You could be going to prison for a long time, Harold. A long time. We're going to arrest you in a minute. Think about that."

Harold just sat there, motionless. "Call Adaline. I'll give you her number and address. Call her."

"Oh, we'll be talking to her," Ken said.

"Call her right now," Harold said, lifting his head and looking at Nicky. His eyes were bloodshot, and he looked like he might cry again. "Call her, so you can confirm it. Then I'll tell you anything you want to know."

Nicky said nothing--only turned around and opened the door.

Harold Smith was a piece of shit. But if his alibi checked out, then he wasn't the killer.

Which meant the real killer was still out there, prowling the streets--maybe hunting his next victim.

CHAPTER TWENTY ONE

Nicky sat in the briefing room at the police station, rubbing her temples in frustration.

Harold Smith's story--as nasty as it was--checked out. Adaline Jones confirmed his alibi. Adaline herself had confessed to her husband, who had confirmed he'd been suspicious for a while, as he worked nights, just like Harold's wife.

Unless Adaline and Harold were conspiring to kill innocent women--which seemed highly ludicrous--then Harold Smith was not their guy.

They'd had no choice but to let him go. Cheating on a wife wasn't a crime. Being a horrible father wasn't a crime. As much as Nicky sometimes wished it could be, these things were just… terrible things that happened sometimes.

The entire thing left a bad taste in her mouth, but she had bigger problems. It was inching closer to one a.m., she was growing tired, and they now had no leads.

She didn't believe this guy was just going to go to sleep and move on with his life. No, at the rate these murders were escalating, Nicky felt sure he'd already have a new subject for his photography--or he was out hunting someone at this very moment.

They needed another lead. They needed anything.

Just then, the door opened, and Nicky looked up to see Ken walking in, the phone to his ear. "Okay... okay, and there's nothing suspicious? Good. Let us know if anything comes up."

Nicky watched as Ken hung up the phone. He let out a sigh and briefly locked eyes with her before sitting down.

"Any news?" Nicky asked.

"The other Harolds seem clean," Ken said. "The officers have nothing to suggest they're involved, and they seem to have solid alibis for the placement of the body."

Damn it. Nicky had thought she'd been onto something with the Harold Smith/Smithson theory, but what if she was wrong? Three men had been cleared now... and here she was, with no other lead to follow down.

"Maybe I was wrong about the name thing," Nicky said. "Maybe it's not somebody named Harold Smith or Smithson."

"It's a lead, though," Ken said. "It's the only lead we have right now. You can't just let it go."

"I'm not letting it go," Nicky said. "I'm just saying--maybe I've been looking at this wrong."

She thought back to what Dr. Graham had said. Nicky did tend to focus too much on one thing. But the name seemed like the ticket.

Maybe it still was... but maybe they were looking at it the wrong way.

She thought of Charles Dumond, the antique store owner, and his new identity. His real name was Richard Fanson, and yet he'd changed his name.

Maybe Harold Smith or Smithson was someone else's name?

Nicky's mind raced down this rabbit hole of thinking. Maybe he was paying homage to someone else named Harold Smith, or maybe he was related to a person with that name? Some other, less obvious way of leaving his mark on the crimes? Nicky wasn't sure... she knew that all of this had to do with art, and photography, and antiques. All of these were hints at the killer's identity. And so were the names.

"What are you thinking, Lyons?" Ken asked.

"I... I think I have an idea," Nicky said. She grabbed her laptop and went online, looking up *Harold Smith, photographer, Florida.*

At first, there weren't any immediate hits. She tried again, this time adding the words art and antique store, then vintage.

That one gained a hit.

The first thing that came up was an article that said: FLORIDA PHOTOGRAPHER HAROLD SMITH, DEAD AT SIXTY-EIGHT.

It was from twenty years ago.

She kept moving through the list and came up with another hit:

HAROLD SMITH, obituary.

Nicky read from the site:

Harold Smith, beloved vintage photographer in the small community of Caledon, Florida, has passed away peacefully at the age of sixty-eight. Survived by his wife, Linda Smith (nee Brooks), and his son, Harrison Smith. Harold was a beloved member of the community who brought joy to others with his talented work.

Contributions in lieu of flowers are to be made to the Caledon Public Library, which was the beneficiary of Harold's will.

Nicky sat back in her chair, reading the words over and over.

Harold Smith.

Harrison Smith.

That was it. Nicky felt it. She looked up at Ken. "It's Harrison Smith," she said.

Ken looked at her, confused. "Harrison Smith?"

"His son, Walker," Nicky said, her pulse racing. "Harold Smith was a semi-famous photographer. He had a kid named Harrison--who should still be alive right now. Caledon is only forty minutes from here."

"Shit," Ken said, grabbing his laptop.

He was finally getting it.

This could be their guy.

"We need to know everything about him," Nicky said. "Most importantly, we need to know where he's living, and if he has a 1998 Hana Kuma."

"I'm on it," Ken said, typing away at his computer.

Nicky began working on her own computer, searching for any and all information about Harrison Smith. She found a few articles, but there was very little information about him online. After digging through a few websites and forums, Nicky learned that Harrison Smith had never left the small community of Caledon, and although he'd tried to get his photography out there, he never picked up the same traction his father did. Vintage photography had become less desirable in the area, and not many people were buying or selling it. Harold Smith's legacy eventually faded, and Harrison never made a name for himself. He also never married or had kids, and his mother died five years after his father did. Professionally, he worked as a janitor.

He fit the profile perfectly. A lonely man with an unfulfilled legacy, a desire to be seen. He was forty-five now, the right age to fit the profile as well.

Nicky got a photo of him from the database. He was a tall, thin, balding man with a bird-like face. Nicky found a phone number and an address.

She felt the adrenaline rush through her veins. This time, it could be for real.

"He has no criminal record," Ken said, "but he does have a car registered in his name."

Nicky lifted her eyes, locking gazes with Ken. He didn't even need to say it.

Harrison Smith had a Hana Kuma.

CHAPTER TWENTY TWO

The bar was full at this hour, just the way he liked it; it made it easier for him to blend in as he sat alone at a table at the back, cradling a glass of scotch. The lights dimmed and the air was smoky and stunk of beer. Trumpets and saxophones played from behind a cordoned-off stage, occasionally letting out a crooning sound that oozed across the room with stunning accuracy. People laughed and talked loudly, glasses clanging together in a rambunctious manner.

There were women here too. So many of them. Most of them too old for his liking. He never chose a subject that looked a day over twenty-five.

There was a brunette with jet black hair sitting at the bar, her back to him. Her long, smooth hair fell in waves, down to her shoulders. There wasn't too much he could see, but he knew what he liked. She wore a red dress that stood out in the crowd, her body curved in just the right way. He'd noticed her when he walked in, but had chosen to wait for the right moment to approach her. He didn't want to look too eager. No need to scare her off. He sipped his drink and tried to compose words in his head, but he had no idea what he was going to say. She turned around and he saw a flash of her face. No... not good enough. She was no model.

His father always had beautiful women as the subject of his photos, and people had adored his work. He clenched his fists. Why did they like his father's work so much, but not appreciate his?

Why was his father so much better?

He felt it wasn't the quality of the work, but rather the nature of an ever-shifting world. Everything was digital now. Back then, people still had an appreciation for classic, vintage photos, but now everything was so fake.

But he wasn't fake. If they wouldn't acknowledge his work, then he would force them to see it.

He smiled against his drink, scanning for another girl to take home. He wanted a brunette... a beautiful brunette, like his mother. His mother was his father's most beloved centerpiece. He took so many photos of her, many of which ended up in magazines.

But his work could be better. He just needed to find the right model. There had to be someone worthy in this bar, somewhere.

He watched a brunette at the bar, and when she turned around, he almost dropped his drink. She was beautiful; her hair was as dark as his, her eyes blue. She was petite, almost child-like. His heart was racing, his palms sweating. She looked young, but there was a hint of maturity in her face. She was the one. He had to have her.

He got up from his table and headed towards her. She was sitting alone. A few men had approached her, but she seemed reluctant to talk to them. He saw an opportunity and took it. The bar was crowded, but he found an empty spot next to her.

"Hi," he said to her, "can I buy you a drink?"

She looked at him for a moment, hesitantly.

"Okay..." she said, and gave him an odd look.

He ordered a drink for her and one for himself. He placed hers in front of her and took a seat. He was trying to think of something to say, but it was hard with her staring at him the way she was.

"What's your name?" he asked.

"Sam."

"I'm Henry." He stuck out his hand to shake hers, and she reluctantly took it. He knew he wasn't the best-looking guy--women had never been too favorable toward him, but he also knew that a nice smile and an offer to buy them a drink could get their attention. They liked confidence, above all else.

And then, when she least expected it, he'd threaten her with a knife and pull her out of the bar, then take her home to immortalize her in a photo.

She'd be so lucky.

"Are you here with anyone?" he asked her as they tried their drinks.

"Yeah." She smiled. "A few friends. I'm celebrating my birthday tonight, so they insisted I come out and have some fun. But they're not here yet."

He reached across the table and grabbed her small hand. "Happy birthday, Sam."

"Thank you." She had a beautiful smile.

"Do you want to dance?" he suddenly asked.

"Oh, no--"

"You don't have to; I just want to get out of here for a minute." He stood up and pulled her hand, trying to be gentle, but firm. He didn't want to scare her.

He led her away from the bar, towards the dance floor. The music was much louder, and the smell of sweat and alcohol was even stronger. He kept pulling her further away from the dance floor and towards the exit at the back, but she kept resisting.

"No, I don’t want to dance," she said. "I'm just going to go back over there now."

But he had her. The music was loud. Even if she tried to scream, they were right by the speakers. No one would hear.

He flashed the knife. Her eyes widened.

"W-what are you doing?"

"I just want to get out of here, okay?" he said. "I'm not gonna hurt you. I just want to talk to you."

He opened the door and she tried to pull away, but he held onto her wrist and dragged her out of the bar, into the back alley. He breathed in the night air, and she struggled, but he kept a firm grip on her. Her hair fell into her face and her blue eyes looked up at him with fear.

"Please let me go," she pleaded. "What do you want from me?"

He didn't answer, just dragged her into the alleyway, where they could finally be alone.

Once he had her, he threw her against the wall and held out the knife. Then, with a smile, he pulled out his camera.

"Why don't we start the shoot early this time?"

CHAPTER TWENTY THREE

Nicky pulled her car up to Harrison Smith's house--an old, farm-style home located on the outskirts of Caledon, Florida. The house loomed on the edge of the dark, empty road, its windows glowing yellow against the night sky. It was surrounded by overgrown grass and trees, with weathered, white paint peeling off its cracked façade. Its chimney sat crooked on the roof, and its wooden shutters hung askew.

It barely looked lived in at all.

"Car's not here," Ken said from the passenger seat, nodding at the driveway.

Nicky's stomach twisted. He was right. And if the car wasn't here, then that could mean Harrison Smith was out hunting his next victim.

"We better check it out anyway, to be sure," Nicky said. The house gave her the creeps, but she needed to be sure Harrison was the right guy, even though she felt in every fiber of her being that he was the killer. But Nicky had been an FBI agent for a long time now, and she knew that sometimes instincts were wrong.

Proof... that was what separated them from the animals.

"Got your gun?" she asked Ken.

"Yep. Let's go."

She turned off the car's engine, and they both climbed out, pulling their guns out of their holsters and heading toward the house.

It was dark as they walked up the driveway. The only light came from the moon, silhouetting the grass and trees around them. The air was warm and still, and there was no sound other than the soft crunch of their shoes on the pebbles.

Nicky's heart was pounding in her chest, and she could hear the blood rushing in her ears. Her hand shook as she pointed her gun at the front door, trying to steady her breathing.

They were almost at the house when Ken suddenly turned and pointed toward the barn. "I'm going to check it out," he said. "Wait here for me."

Nicky opened her mouth to protest, but Ken was already walking toward the barn. The door was wide open, casting out a rectangle of light into the dark yard. Moments later, Ken came back out and jogged over.

"No sign of the car over there either."

"He might not be home," Nicky said, glancing at the door. "Let's knock anyway."

She banged on the front door of the house--only for it to creak open beneath her fist.

Nicky and Ken exchanged a look.

It was unlocked, as she expected. She pushed on the door and walked in.

The front hall was dimly lit by a dusty chandelier, and Nicky raised her hand to her brow to shield her eyes from the low light. Halfway up the hall, she noticed a doorway leading to the living room.

"Hello? Mr. Smith?" Nicky called out. "It's the FBI. We just want to ask you a few questions."

She heard Ken walking around in the living room, opening up the drapes to let in more light. Nicky walked across the hall and peered in. Ken was standing in front of a large armchair in the center of the room. His posture looked stiff and tense, and he was sweating.

Then, Nicky saw it too: the armchair...

It was the same as one of the ones in the photo. Nicky's stomach churned.

She could see the blood and everything.

She pulled out her phone--she needed to call this in and get police down here, now. The operator picked up immediately, and Nicky said, "This is Agent Lyons of the FBI, we have a situation at 4012 Sullivan Road in Caledon. Requesting immediate backup and forensics--we might have a crime scene. Requesting an APB for one Harrison Smith of Caledon, Florida, wanted under suspicion of homicide."

"Copy that, Agent Lyons," the operator said. "Backup is on its way and the APB is being put out."

"Thank you," Nicky said, hanging up.

"It's him, isn't it?" Ken asked, still staring at the chair.

"I think so," Nicky said. "Let's keep looking, though."

Ken nodded and crossed the room. Nicky followed him down the hallway, glancing into a few rooms on the left and right.

"I'll take the upstairs," Ken said. "You check the basement."

"Got it."

Nicky made her way down the stairs to the basement. It was dark and dusty down here, with cobwebs in the corners. The basement was mostly empty, save for a workbench in the corner and some boxes.

But when she turned a corner, her blood ran cold.

There, right in front of her, was a makeshift photography studio set up, equipped with a tripod and all. A vintage floral couch, the one seen in the photos, and blood stains all over the concrete floor.

There was no doubt about it now.

This was their guy. They were in the killer's house--but he wasn't home.

Which meant, chances were, he was out hunting right now.

Nicky's mind raced. They needed to catch him now--but an APB wasn't enough. It might not get a hit. No, she needed something more concrete.

Running up the stairs, she met with Ken on the main level.

"He's not here," Ken said.

"No, but his little photo studio is," Nicky said, gesturing to the basement.

"Jesus," Ken said, pale and sickly-looking.

Nicky took out her phone and called Grace's number. Within a few rings, Grace picked up with a yawn. "Nicky--"

"Grace, I know it's late, but I need you again."

"I'm not tired, I swear! What's up?"

"I need you to track someone down for me. Maybe triangulate cell data or use GPS if you have to."

"I might be able to do that," Grace said. "Who am I hunting?"

"Harrison Smith of Caledon, Florida. He's not home right now, but we need to find him." Nicky took a breath. "Grace, he's the killer."

"Holy crap," Grace said. "Give me a minute, let me see what I can do."

Nicky heard keys clacking on the other end of the line. She bit her lip and paced the house, just as she heard police cars coming up to the house outside. She peeked out the window to see officers arriving. Then, she glanced around the house, at the creepy old wallpaper, the old vintage photos--Harold Smith, Harrison's father's, work.

She paused on a photo of a brunette woman--who looked eerily similar to the girls Harrison had been taking. His mother, maybe? Her gut twisted with disgust.

Eventually, Grace came back on: "I've pinned his location down to a community called Pleasantview. It's small, barely even a town, but they have a popular bar there that brings in patrons from other towns, a little upscale. Very rich area. The bar closes at three a.m."

That was Harrison's M.O. He liked rich, pretty, young girls, and he was on the hunt for another one.

"Send me the address," Nicky said.

"Already in your email."

"Thanks." Nicky hung up, and then she turned to Ken. "We've got an address." She hesitated. "Are you coming?"

"Of course, I am," Ken said. "You're going to need someone with an extra gun."

She nodded and headed for the door. As they were leaving the house, the officers were running in. Nicky didn't have time to explain it all, but she stopped one officer and said, "We need forensics in there now."

"Yes, ma'am!"

Nicky and Ken hurried over to Nicky's car. But just as Nicky was about to get in--her phone rang.

She pulled it out, standing under the clear night sky.

It was Chief Schmitt.

"Chief?" Nicky asked. What would he be calling her for?

"Lyons, we have a situation."

Nicky faced Ken across the hood of the car. He couldn't hear her call from this distance, but she was sure her expression told him something was not good.

"What's going on, Chief?"

"It's the Smith man, Harold--the guy you two brought in, then released... we just got a call about him..."

Nicky's chest sank and her blood ran cold. "What happened?"

"His nanny just called 911. Apparently, he's holding his child and his wife hostage in their garage, threatening to kill them with a knife." Chief Schmitt paused. "The nanny's trying to talk him down and stall for time, but he's demanding to talk to you and Agent Walker."

"Fuck," Nicky said. "I can't be there,

"Lyons, we have a woman and infant's life on the line here--"

"I know," Nicky cut in.

But *damn.* She had to go get Harrison Smith. She couldn't go back to Harold's house and deal with this, not when there was a killer on the loose. The weight of the decision made Nicky's head spin. What was she supposed to do? Nicky and Ken couldn't be in two places at once. There was only one option:

"I'll send Walker alone," she said. "Maybe he can talk Smith down by himself."

"You better hope he can, Lyons."

The chief hung up, and Nicky took a breath as she looked up at Ken.

"That sounded bad," he said.

Nicky sighed. This night--this whole damn day--could not get any worse. "I need you to go back to Harold Smith's house; he's holding his wife and kid hostage."

"What?" Ken asked, his face falling. "You can't be serious. I don't wanna leave you--"

"I'm ok," Nicky said. "Please, Ken. Go back there, talk to them, and save them. I'll go get Harrison--and then we'll meet back up later. We can handle this."

Ken looked like he wanted to protest, but he must have realized that he couldn't. Nicky couldn't afford to wait around if she wanted to catch the killer.

"I'll be back as soon as I can," Ken said. "I promise."

Nicky nodded and watched as Ken walked away. He went to talk to a police officer about borrowing one of their cars; then he got into a car and drove off down the street, away from her. Nicky's heart twisted as she watched him go, and she chastised herself for letting her personal feelings get in the way.

Nicky couldn't afford to get distracted now. She had a killer to hunt.

CHAPTER TWENTY FOUR

The drive to Pleasantview was quick, but Nicky's heart was pounding the whole time. She kept imagining the worst--Harrison, the killer, the psychopath whatever the hell he was, killing someone else. Another innocent girl's life stolen from her for no reason other than some psycho's sick, deranged fame fantasy.

She had to stop him.

When she pulled into town, Nicky could see that it was upscale and beautiful. The trees lining the streets were huge, towering oaks and pines. The houses were old, stately homes, complete with manicured lawns, lavish gardens, and expensive cars parked along the curb.

This was it, the kind of place that Harrison Smith would gravitate toward to find a victim.

Nicky had arranged for local police to be patrolling the town looking for him, while she would infiltrate the bar. Nicky made her way toward downtown, racing as fast as her car would safely take her, and skidded up to the curb. She hopped out to see a fairly vacant downtown street, but through the windows of the bar, it was surprisingly lively.

Nicky stood on the curb, in front of the bar, and took a breath. Then she made her way up the sidewalk to the front door, and pushed it open to the bar.

The interior was dim and smoky, filled with young people enjoying the nightlife, and a live band played on a small stage against the far wall.

Nicky made her way through the crowd, looking for Harrison. Was he here? Had he arrived yet? She couldn't see him, but she was on his tail.

"Hey, lady!" someone called, and Nicky turned to see a red-headed woman in a white halter top and short skirt standing before her, in the middle of the bar. She held a drink and had an annoyed expression on her face. "Do you mind?"

Nicky looked down and realized she was standing in the middle of the woman's dance floor. "Sorry!" she said and ducked out of the way.

She moved to the edge of the bar and scanned the room over the crowd. No sign of Harrison. Where the hell was he? She locked eyes with the bartender, who took notice of her, coming over to serve her a drink as if she were any patron.

"What can I get ya, miss?"

Nicky subtly flashed her badge. She didn't want to make a scene. The bartender's eyes widened.

"What is this?" he asked.

"I'm looking for a man," Nicky said, glancing around the room, then back at the bartender. "Lanky build, white." She quickly took out her phone and flashed a photo of Harrison.

The bartender looked at it, squinting. "Yeah, I seen him. He bought a young lady a drink not long ago."

Blood rushed to Nicky's skull. No--she might already be too late. *Not again.*

"Where are they now?" Nicky asked.

"No idea, I haven't seen them since they bought a drink," he said.

"And when was that, exactly?" Nicky pressed. "Please. This is extremely important."

The man swallowed nervously. "Well, I'd say it was fifteen minutes ago or so."

"Thank you." With that, Nicky dashed through the bar, looking through the sea of faces for any sign of Harrison Smith. There were too many people, and it disoriented her.

She pushed through the crowd, making her way to the back of the room and toward the bathrooms, when she heard yelling coming from somewhere nearby and outside.

Nicky turned and saw a waitress leading a young woman into a back room. No sign of Harrison.

She turned back to the crowd, desperation setting in. She had to find him before it was too late. But where could he be?

Suddenly, Nicky felt a draft hit her legs from somewhere in the bar. She looked to see that the back door, leading to an alley behind, was slightly ajar.

Bingo.

Nicky darted to the door and pushed it open to find herself in a dark alley behind the bar. The wind was whipping, and as soon as Nicky stepped out, she could see a figure standing in the distance, facing away.

"Smith!" Nicky called. "Harrison Smith, you're under arrest."

The figure froze, and Nicky whipped her gun out, pointing it at his back. As she got closer, she realized that the man was holding something in his hands--a camera.

And in front of him, pressed against a wall, was a young brunette woman.

"Do. Not. Move," Nicky ordered. "Harrison Smith, this is the FBI. Move and I'll shoot."

"H-help me!" the girl cried.

Nicky's blood raced in her veins. She had Harrison, at last. And now she would make him pay for what he had done to all those innocent women.

Slowly, she stepped toward him, keeping her gun trained on his back. Her heart pounded with fury as she finally closed in on him, ready to take him down once and for all.

But when she was just inches away from Harrison, he suddenly turned around and pulled out a knife. Nicky gasped as the blade glinted in the dim light of the alleyway.

"You're not taking me," Harrison snarled, his eyes wild with rage and fear.

Nicky raised her gun and fired, but Harrison moved quickly, and the bullet missed. Before Nicky could react, Harrison had the victim--and he was holding the knife to her throat. The victim whimpered, and Harrison's eyes locked on Nicky's like a violent animal.

No.

Nicky raised her gun and took a step back, knowing that if this was going to end, it would have to be on her terms.

She kept her gaze locked on Harrison's as they circled each other in the alleyway, their eyes burning with hatred and desperation. For a moment, Nicky wondered if it was even worth it--if this man could ever truly be brought to justice for what he had done to so many innocent women.

But then she saw the look of sheer evil in Harrison's eyes and knew that this was the only way things could end between them. She couldn't let him get away again--not with the stakes so high.

If she was going to save this girl, she might have to shoot to kill.

CHAPTER TWENTY FIVE

Ken had been in a lot of messed up situations during his career as an FBI agent. But dealing with a man who was threatening to kill his own wife and infant son? This was another level of crazy, and Ken wasn't sure his stomach could handle it.

Driving in a police officer's car, he finally reached Harold Smith's residence--where he saw a series of police cars parked out front, and a few officers talking at the closed garage, one with a megaphone. Ken whipped the car up to the curb, threw it in park, and hurried over to the officers.

"Agent Walker, you're here," Chief Schmitt said.

"I got here as soon as I could," Ken said. "What the hell is going on?"

"Bastard's threatening to kill his wife and kid, said he'll only talk to you and Agent Lyons."

Off to the side, Margaret, the old nanny, was shaking like a leaf, but she trotted over. "Oh, Agent, it's terrible! Mr. Smith has completely lost it--where is Agent Lyons?"

"She couldn't make it, ma'am," Ken said.

"Oh, dear." Margaret shook her head. "Well, I can't explain it, but it's like he's some kind of monster. He told me to go home, and then I heard screaming--and then this."

"His wife and kid are in the house right now?" he asked.

"Yes, sir," Schmitt said. "In the garage. We've got the place surrounded, and we're trying to call him, to try and talk him down--but he keeps saying he'll only talk to you."

"I'll do what I can," Ken said. "But we can't let him hurt his family. We need to get them out of there, now."

Schmitt handed him the megaphone, and Ken faced the garage. Every officer on the scene was pale and tense, Ken included. One wrong move could mean the death of a baby and an innocent woman.

Ken could not--would not--have that blood on his hands.

"Harold, are you in there?" Ken said into the megaphone.

A moment of silence, and Harold's voice sounded through the garage door. "Agent Walker, I'm here," he said. "Where is Agent Lyons? I need her here too."

"She's on her way, I promise," Ken said, a blatant lie, but he just needed to talk Harold down. "Talk to me, Harold. What's going on here?"

"It's... it's my Adaline..."

Ken frowned. The woman Harold was cheating with?

"When you called her to confirm my alibi, she... she told her husband everything, and then, and then..." A choking sound. "She left me, damn it! It's over between us, and she left me with this--this woman, and this stupid child I don't even want!"

A woman's cry came out from the other side of the garage, along with the disgruntled coo of the baby, JJ.

"Oh God, Harold," the woman said. "What are you doing?"

"Get off me!" Harold's voice was louder now.

"Harold, please, don't do this. It's not worth it," she said, her voice cracking. "I love you. I want to fix this. We can get through this together."

Harold laughed, hollow and cruel. "I don't want you, Maggie, I want Adaline, but because of these stupid FBI agents, I'll never have her!"

Ken saw where this was going. Harold blamed Ken and Nicky for his affair going south, and now he was lashing out. This was a highly volatile, dangerous man, and Ken wished Nicky was here to use her compassionate side to get through to him--but this was on Ken now. He had to talk Harold down.

"C'mon, Harold, you don't mean that," Ken said. "You have a wife, and she's in there with you. You don't want to hurt Maggie and JJ, Harold. They're innocent. If you want to hurt me and Agent Lyons, well, I guess I understand that, but you don't have to hurt the others. They had nothing to do with this."

"I want Agent Lyons here, now," Harold said. "She's the reason Adaline left me, and I want to make her pay."

"You're right, Harold," Ken said. "I'm sorry--that's our fault, and we'll do everything we can to fix it. But if you hurt Maggie, you'll never get Adaline back. We both know that."

"I don't care!" Harold's voice echoed through the garage.

"It's too late for that now, Agent Walker. And I can't let them go. I can't let them ruin my life. I'm going to kill them all."

Ken's veins ran cold. This was not going well.

"Harold, you can't kill your wife," Ken said, trying to keep his voice calm and even. "Think about JJ. He's innocent here, Harold--you're his father. You don't want to kill your own son."

"I don't care about that stupid kid!" Harold snarled. "I don't care about any of them! If I can't have Adaline, I don't want anyone!"

"If you kill them, Harold, it'll destroy you," Ken said. "You'll destroy you, and you'll destroy your family."

"It will be their own damn fault for destroying my life!" Harold yelled. "I won't let them do this to me. I won't let you do this to me. I'm going to kill them all!"

Ken looked up at the tense police officers around him, and then back at the garage door.

"Harold, I know you're confused," he said. "But I just want you to know that no one's gonna judge you if you just walk out of that door right now. Open the garage, Harold. Come on out and talk. We'll get Adaline over here too. We can work this out. No one has to die."

"No!" Harold's voice grew louder. "No, you want to take away the one thing I want in life! You want me to take a vow of chastity and raise some kid I don't even want? No, I won't do that! The FBI can't force me to do that! And if they try, they'll have to answer to me!"

Ken's heart was pounding. "Harold, please, don't do this," he said. "Just walk out of there now. No one has to die here."

"I'm going to kill you, Agent Walker," Harold said. "Then I'll kill Agent Lyons, and I'll kill Maggie and JJ, and then I'll kill myself, and I'll be with Adaline in hell! And no one will be able to stop me!"

"Harold, please, don't do this," Ken said. "Don't let this happen. You wanna kill me? Fine, go ahead! Come out and fucking kill me, man, but leave Maggie and the baby out of it!"

Silence on the other side of the garage made Ken's blood run like ice. He held his breath. But when he heard a whimper from Maggie and a sound from the baby, he let out that breath. They were still alive.

He could still do this.

"Harold, can you hear me, buddy?" Ken called out.

"Yeah... yeah, I'm here." His voice was thick with tears now. This gave Ken hope. Hope that Harold would find a heart in himself and come out of this.

"Please, Harold," Ken said. "Come on out. Deal with me face-to-face. Leave your family out of it. How does that sound?"

"B-but, if I come out, you'll shoot me," Harold said.

"I promise, Harold, no one's gonna hurt you," Ken said. He hoped the officers would abide by that too. If Harold would just come out without hurting anyone, then Ken would see to it that he'd be treated fairly and not harmed.

"Okay... okay, I... I'll come out," Harold said.

Ken didn't know if Harold would do that, but he and the officers formed a semi-circle in front of the garage door, rifles trained on the door.

Ken raised his megaphone. "Okay Harold, just open the door, and we'll be right there, man-to-man. No one has to go to jail here. Just open the door, and we'll talk about it."

The garage door shifted. It began to slowly open, revealing Harold holding a knife to Maggie's throat, and the baby on the floor next to them.

"Okay, Harold, let's just talk about this," Ken said as he slowly walked into the garage.

Not a single officer moved. They stood outside, and Harold stood in the garage, with his wife and his son and his knife, and Ken.

No one moved.

"Is this what you want, Harold?" Ken asked as he approached Harold. "You want me here, so you can kill me?"

"Yes," Harold said.

"Okay, then that's what we'll do," Ken said. "I'm here, Harold. You want me to die, you can kill me. But I'm not gonna move any closer, and you can't do anything to Maggie and JJ. Let Maggie go."

"If I do that, you'll shoot me," Harold said.

"We won't shoot," Ken promised. "Just drop the knife and let Maggie and the baby go."

Harold's eyes were filled with tears, but he shook his head. "No. If I let them go, you'll take them from me."

"Harold, please," Ken said. "You don't want to keep doing this. You want me to die, you can do that. But let Maggie and JJ go."

Harold shook his head. "No. I want them to die too."

"I won't let that happen," Ken said. "I'll shoot myself before I let that happen."

"I'll shoot you first," Harold said.

"Harold, let's just talk about this," Ken said. "What do you want to do? Do you want me to die? Do you want Maggie and JJ to live? Just tell me, and I'll make it happen."

"I want Adaline back," Harold said. "I want her to come back, and I want her to be happy with me. I'm going to kill you and Agent Lyons. And then I'm going to kill Maggie and JJ. And then I'm going to kill myself, and I'll be with Adaline in hell, and no one will be able to stop me."

"Harold, I'm here," Ken said. "You want to end this, here's your chance. Let her go, and I'll come closer. We'll work this out. We can find a way to fix this, Harold."

"No, it's too late for that," Harold said.

"No, it's not too late," Ken said. "It's not too late to turn this around, Harold. It's not too late to save your family. Just drop the knife."

"You son of a bitch!" Harold spat, and shoved Maggie away.

In that split-second, Ken saw Maggie's eyes flash with terror, but she was free. She swept down and grabbed the baby, then ran out of the garage, to Ken's relief--but then Harold lunged at Ken with the knife.

"Don't shoot!" Ken shouted at the other officers, who were standing by, ready to fire. He dodged Harold's attack, and thankfully, the officers listened to his order.

They could do this without bloodshed. Ken didn't want to kill Harold. The man clearly needed help, and he thought about Nicky, and how compassionate she'd been with Mr. Dumond earlier. Ken knew that, sometimes, he could use some of that compassion himself.

So, he wouldn't kill Harold Smith. He just had to get the upper hand on him and cuff him.

Ken dodged Harold's attack and grabbed him from behind, trying to subdue him. Harold's knife-hand came up, and Ken saw a flash of yellow and black, and suddenly he felt a sharp, searing pain in his forearm. The knife slashed into him.

"Agent Walker!" Chief Schmitt cried out. "Get out of the way, we're gonna shoot!"

"Don't shoot!" Ken shouted. He grunted out in pain, but he didn't let go. He just tightened his grip and struggled with Harold to bring him down. He managed to get Harold to drop the knife, then shoved him back. Harold stumbled back against the wall, and Ken pressed his advantage. He lunged at Harold and grabbed the knife before Harold could react. Then he wrestled Harold to the floor, and pinned him, whipping out his handcuffs. Harold writhed beneath him, but couldn't get away.

"It's over, Harold," Ken said. "It's all over."

As Ken slapped the cuffs on Harold, he just hoped Nicky was having the same luck with the killer.

CHAPTER TWENTY SIX

Harrison Smith had his knife pressed to the victim's throat, and Nicky could see it: She was seconds away from total failure. In a quick slash, Harrison could end this woman's life.

She could not let that happen.

Facing off against him in the alleyway, the moonlight shone down and glimmered against Harrison's blade. Nicky held her gun firm, but her palms were sweaty.

"Drop the knife, Harrison," Nicky said. "It doesn't have to end this way."

In his eyes, Nicky saw no soul. He didn't show a hint of emotion as he gripped the woman tighter. She was sure the only thing holding him back from killing her was the knowledge that he would be shot dead on sight if he tried.

"You don't understand anything," Harrison said. "I won't let you ruin my greatest creation before it's even complete."

"It's over, Harrison," Nicky said. "Drop the knife and I can take you in peacefully. No one has to die here, Harrison."

She slowly inched closer as she spoke. The FBI had trained her to deal with tense situations, life or death situations, but being in one of them never felt easier when the stakes were so high, so real.

Nicky grasped her gun tighter still. She had no idea what would happen if she shot Harrison, but she knew that she had to try.

"I think it's you who doesn't understand the situation you're in," Harrison said. "I'm not going to prison for the rest of my life. I'm not going to be locked up! No! I'm not done yet!"

His voice was getting louder, more unstable. Fear filled Nicky's chest as she saw the woman in Harrison's grip move her arm. She was trying to protect herself from Harrison's insane plans. But Nicky shot her a look--a piercing look that said *don't move.* The girl whimpered but obliged. The worst thing she could do was try to get herself out.

But if Nicky couldn't save her, she would never be able to live with the guilt.

She stepped closer into the light. When Harrison saw Nicky, a different look flashed across his face--a more deranged, crazed look.

"My, my, you're quite the beauty yourself," he said, grinning. "A little bit older than what I usually go for, but yes, I could make you work. Perhaps I should take your picture instead."

"Drop the knife, Harrison," Nicky said.

No. No, no, no. This was not how it was supposed to happen. Nicky was going to take Harrison down. She was going to save the woman. Everything was going to be okay.

He was not supposed to be the one making her feel the fear.

"Drop the knife," Nicky said. "You're surrounded, Harrison. Drop it and you'll be taken in peacefully."

Harrison let out a short, shrill laugh. "You think I'm afraid of you?" he said. "You think it's that easy? You're not going to do anything to stop me."

Shit. Nicky needed to switch her tactic fast. She needed to get into his head. What did she know about Harrison Smith? He was a delusional narcissist, living in the shadow of his father's forgotten legacy. All he wanted was to be known for his photography--by any means necessary.

This was a person who had no fear, and who wouldn't give up without a fight.

But he'd said something she could use. He thought she would work for his "art."

Nicky was willing to do anything to save this girl. So, she said, "Fine then, you win, Harrison."

His eyes flashed. "What?"

"You win," she said. "I know you need to finish your work, and to do that, you need a worthy subject. So, take me. Leave that girl and take me instead."

Harrison laughed again. "You don't know what you're asking for."

"I know exactly what I'm asking for," she said. "I'm asking for you to let her go, and for you to take me instead."

"No."

"You need someone who is willing to go the distance for your work," Nicky said. "Someone who will let you photograph them in ways that would make your father proud. Someone who isn't afraid to go to the dark depths of hell for your art."

Harrison laughed, and Nicky could see him loosening his grip on the girl--beginning to let his guard down.

"What?" he said again.

Nicky was bluffing. She had no idea how to rescue this girl, but she needed to buy herself more time--to make Harrison think she was on his side, to make him lower his guard.

"I'm a photographer, too," Nicky said. "I'd make a great subject, Harrison. You can even make me your next muse. You can take all the pictures you want; you can do all the things you want. But first, let the girl go. Let her get out of here."

"No way," Harrison said. "I need her for my work. She's my muse."

"I'm your muse," Nicky said, taking a step closer. "Let her go. You know you want to."

His grip loosened on the woman.

Nicky waltzed even closer.

"You can have me," she said. "I'm yours. I'll do whatever you want."

"You're lying," he said. "You wouldn't really let me take you, would you?"

He was weakening. She could see the cracks in his façade.

"I would," Nicky said. "I'd let you take me. Take my picture. Make me your muse. But only if you let her go."

"I could do that," he said. "I could do all those things to you. I could make you my next muse."

"Then let her go," Nicky said. "If you want me, let her go."

She was close enough to lunge at him now. All she had to do was make her move.

"Let her go, Harrison," she said. "Let her go and take me instead."

"You won't really go," he countered.

"I will," she said. "If it means saving her, I'll do anything to save her."

He looked over at the girl. And then, in a flash, he dropped her to the ground and lunged for Nicky. Everything moved in a blur after that.

The girl screamed, and Nicky could hear her footsteps pounding the pavement, the sound of Harrison's breathing getting closer, louder.

She aimed the gun forward, but he was too close.

She fired.

She missed.

He dodged.

She fired again.

And again.

He kept coming, and Nicky knew she was in trouble.

She fired a fourth shot, this time hitting his arm. His knife dropped to the ground and slid away.

And then he was on her.

Nicky felt her gun go flying from her hand. The force of his body pushed her back against a brick wall. When she looked up, Harrison's eyes were wild. His hand went around her throat. He squeezed.

Nicky could feel herself starting to fade. But she could still fight. She could still fight for this girl, for herself, for all the people who were depending on her.

She reached up and grabbed Harrison's hand and struggled to push it away from her neck. She threw her knee up, kicking him violently in the groin, just hard enough to knock the wind from him. Nicky scrambled to her feet and went to grab her gun--but Harrison took the moment to flee. He dashed in the direction of the road.

"Oh no you don't!" Securing her gun, Nicky ran after him until they hit the main road. Harrison dashed forward, and then, Nicky saw it: the 1998 Hana Kuma. Harrison's car.

His long legs carried him fast, and he was at the car in seconds. Nicky fired off a shot at him, but he ducked and got into the car. She went to fire again--but she was out of bullets. She had to reload. She went to pull a mag out, but it was too late--Harrison's car started.

He whipped out of the parking spot and turned--coming straight for Nicky. The headlights momentarily blinded her, and she dodged out of the way, landing in a pile of garbage bags.

She could hear his tires screeching from behind her, and she jumped up just in time to see Harrison's car pulling away--leaving her behind. The car squealed, and then Harrison was off down the road, speeding away.

She ran after it--but it was no use. He was gone.

Nicky spotted her own car up ahead, parked at the side of the road too.

There was only one option left.

She was going after him herself--and she'd do it by car.

CHAPTER TWENTY SEVEN

Nicky's car was an old, beat-up junker. It wasn't much, but it got her where she needed to go--and it had been with her since college, so it held a special place in her heart.

But that didn't stop her from yanking the steering wheel and turning on a dime as soon as she got into the driver's seat. She slammed it into reverse and pulled out--tires screeching. Then she turned the wheel again, and floored the little car.

She knew she'd have to be quick if she was going to catch up to him. He had a head-start, and even though his car was a shit-box, it was still ahead of hers.

The window in the car was open, and Nicky could feel the wind whipping in around her. He was driving fast, but she was going faster. It was the only way to catch up to him. She had to get there faster.

She could hear his car in the distance. It was just a matter of time now. She was going to catch him.

The next few minutes were a blur. Nicky barely registered the twists and turns they took through the city. She had to stay focused. She had to remember the paths they took, the turns they made. She had to be sure she knew where he was going.

It was difficult to tell how far ahead he was, but the sound of his car grew louder and louder. Nicky found herself on the stretch of highway that led out of town--and there, up ahead, she saw him.

Harrison's Hana Kuma.

Nicky pressed harder on the gas pedal. There was no one else on the road--just him and her, flying through the outskirts, past farmland.

She watched as the road curved, and she followed. Her tires squealed as she made the turn, and her car started to sway. She had to hold on. She had to keep it on the road. She couldn't lose him now.

She pressed even harder on the gas pedal. Harrison was speeding too, until both of them were going so fast their cars were shaking. Nicky wasn't sure how much of a beating her old car could take--but she knew for sure Harrison's 1998 hunk of junk couldn't handle much more.

Nicky's car was going faster and faster. She could feel her heart pounding in her chest. She wasn't sure if that was because of the speed, or because of what she was about to do.

She just knew she had to catch up to him. She had to end it.

Harrison's car was just ahead. She could see it better now as she got closer. It was practically falling apart. It had a giant dent in the side and the back looked like it had been crumpled in a ball.

Then--a loud POP. Harrison blew a tire. She slammed on the breaks, causing her car to screech to a halt. The tires squealed and the car shook--but she held it on the road. This would be the end of it.

Nicky watched as Harrison's car flew right at a pole, slamming into it, head-first. Nicky threw her door open and dashed at the wreckage as smoke piled into the air.

She ran and ran, her shoes kicking up dust. Then she reached the car and stopped. Her heart was pounding. Her breaths were short.

She stood there and looked at it, smoke still pouring into the air. When she was sure he wasn't getting out of it, she started walking around the car. Her gun was in her hand, and she aimed it at the car, just in case.

But it was empty.

The door was open. There was no one inside.

She walked around the car and looked through the passenger window--and that's when she saw him.

He was there, on the ground, crawling on the asphalt. He was holding his head. His leg was bleeding.

She looked down at the gun in her hand, and then back at him. For a moment, she had a suspicion that he was going for a gun of his own, that he had one on him and he'd pull it out any second now and fire at her. But she looked at him, and she saw how injured he was. He was stuck. He wasn't moving.

He just kept trying to crawl.

"That's far enough, Harrison," Nicky said. "It's over."

He looked back at her. His eyes were wild. He looked like a cornered animal.

He coughed. His eyes were starting to close. He was going to pass out.

"It's over, Harrison," Nicky said. "I'm here to bring you in."

She stepped closer to him. He was still on the ground, just a few feet away from her.

"I'm not going to prison," he said, his voice quivering. "I'll die first."

"You're not going to die, Harrison," Nicky said. "Just put your hands up where I can see them."

She half-expected him to grab a gun and start firing. She wouldn't have been surprised. She knew she had to be careful.

But he didn't. He just lay there, on the ground.

"Please, Harrison," Nicky said. "I don't want to shoot you. Just give yourself up."

He didn't respond. She could see it then. He was done. He was done fighting, done resisting.

This was it.

As Nicky was getting closer to him, still holding her gun firmly, she reached for her handcuffs. Harrison was done--she was sure of it. But as she was getting closer, he threw his leg out and attempted to knock Nicky over.

But she was ready for it. She jumped over his swipe, then landed beside him and kicked him hard in the stomach.

"I said it's over, Harrison!" Nicky screamed. "Don't make me shoot you!"

He deserved to rot in prison. She wouldn't let him take the easy way out.

"No..." Harrison whimpered. "No, it can't be over... I wasn't done... I needed to take more pictures..."

"You'll never take another picture again." She kept her gun pointed at him, along with her deadly gaze.

"I didn't... I never understood why they all liked my father's work so much, but wouldn't even look at mine... why? Why? Why wasn't I good enough?"

A key trait of narcissism was a deep insecurity at one's core. Nicky knew that was what they were dealing with here.

"We make our own worth in life, Harrison," Nicky said. "You chose to live in your father's shadow. You could have been your own person, but you wasted your life."

"It wasn't supposed to be like this..." Harrison continued. "I was supposed to be the great one... I was supposed to make them all feel the way they made me feel..."

"A lot of people don't get the recognition they think they deserve," Nicky said. "But it doesn't make them evil."

"I'm not evil... I'm not..."

"Of course, you are," Nicky said. "You killed four people. Four innocent women who had lives and hopes and dreams. Do you know what that makes you?"

"I... I can't go to prison..."

"You're a murderer, Harrison," Nicky said, her voice full of disgust. "You're a sick, twisted, evil person."

She watched him lying on the ground, a look of fear on his face. He was defeated. She could tell. He wasn't going to get up again.

"I'm not evil..." Harrison's voice was soft now. He was struggling to stay conscious. "I just... I just wanted to be taken seriously... I just wanted..."

Nicky had enough of this. "Get up," she said, "or I'll shoot you right now."

He looked back at her. He was defeated. She could see it in his eyes. He was done.

Slowly, he lifted himself up. He was holding his stomach.

"Put your hands behind your back," she said.

She watched as he did it. She cuffed him, then she grabbed him by the arm and started dragging him to her car.

"You're going to jail," she said. "I'm taking you in. Don't say another word."

She opened the door and made him get inside. Then she slammed the door and walked around to the driver's side.

Harrison Smith was a deranged lunatic. He'd killed four women, maybe even more.

But now, he'd never hurt anyone else again.

CHAPTER TWENTY EIGHT

When Nicky walked into the briefing room at the FBI HQ in Jacksonville, she was surprised to see no one was there. The morning light slashed through the windows and fell across the floor, reflecting off the shiny surface and blinding her eyes. The long table of the room, with its many chairs, brought back so many memories for her. Memories of when she was first put in charge of the task force to find those missing girls.

Memories of her successes--and her failures.

Harrison Smith had been taken into custody. The amount of evidence against him was overwhelming, and Nicky knew this trial was already done and over with before it even began. He was a killer.

He'd get life.

The bodies of the girls he'd killed were found in his basement, stuffed into boxes and left to rot, as though they weren't human beings at all. The entire thing made Nicky want to crawl into herself and hide forever; she was grateful to have stopped Harrison but devastated she hadn't been able to save the girls he'd killed.

Paris Conner was on their list. If they'd looked sooner, or tried harder, would they have been able to prevent her death?

Nicky knew it was pointless to dwell on things she couldn't change. Dr. Graham would tell her that, of course, but she had to remember it herself sometimes, too.

All she could do was push forward, and try to save more people, and hope maybe her life would bring more good than harm to a cruel and often unjust world.

The door opened, and Nicky looked over her shoulder to see Ken. His blue eyes were bright in the sunlight, and he had a relaxed posture, with his hands in the pockets of his tanned slacks.

"Hey, you're here early for once," he said.

Nicky couldn't help but smile. She was happy to hear everything had worked out on his end too. He'd been able to talk the father down from killing his family and help him get the psychiatric care he needed.

For the most part, things did work out.

Ken walked closer to Nicky, and she walked closer to him. Before she could react, he pulled her into a hug, holding her tight in his arms. Nicky relaxed into him, feeling safe.

"I'm glad you're okay," he said.

"You too." She held him tighter.

They pulled away. Nicky looked up and locked eyes with Ken. His eyes fluttered to her lips, and her heart swelled--just as the door opened, and Chief Franco filed in with Grace. Nicky and Ken stepped away from each other lightning fast, but Nicky could tell by the look on Grace--and the chief's--faces that they had seen the whole thing. Face hot, Nicky bowed at the chief and sat down.

"Lyons, Walker, Taylor," Franco said as everyone took their spots. He stood at the head of the table. "Good work. This guy was about to go on an even more violent killing spree, and you managed to stop it."

"Thank you, sir," Nicky and Ken both said, in unison.

Nicky felt her face burn. She knew she was only going to make it worse.

"And I'm glad all of you are okay," Franco said. "You were lucky to survive that. And I commend how quickly you got this done, however..."

Nicky swallowed hard. She knew what was coming next.

"We still lost a lot of girls," he said. "I wish we had put Paris Conner at the forefront of our list, but the truth is, we didn't even know where we were looking until that picture came in." The chief sighed. "It is a lot of bloodshed, though."

"I know, chief." Nicky lowered her head in shame.

"Lyons, you've been with me for years," the chief said. "You know that there's no way we could have known. I wish we had gone in sooner, and maybe we could have prevented a couple of these deaths, but you can't blame yourself for this."

"Thank you, sir." Nicky nodded.

"That being said," Franco said. "I think it goes to show that this is our job. We have to stop people like Harrison Smith before they have the chance to do anything. I think we all learned that lesson, and I think we have to make sure it doesn't happen again."

"I agree, sir," Nicky said.

"We're not going to let it stop us now," Franco said. "We're going to keep looking, and we're going to keep trying to save these other girls. Our resolve hasn't weakened. If anything, it has to be stronger. You agree, right, Lyons?"

Nicky nodded eagerly. "Of course, sir."

"Good. You're the leader of this team. There are still more girls on that list--and I'm trusting you to find and save them."

Nicky felt her chest swell with pride. She was grateful for this--and grateful to have the support of her team. She wouldn't take this for granted. No—from now on, Nicky was sure of it—she would save more girls.

"Thank you, sir."

"Good. Now take the day off to recoup, then we're back at it again."

With that, Franco left. Nicky felt her chest rise and fall with the breath she took, and she let it out slowly. She looked up at Ken, who was already looking at her.

Franco's words kept playing through her head.

She had to save the girls. She was the one who knew about this. It was up to her to stop it.

She had to live up to the chief's faith in her. To her team's faith in her, and her faith in herself.

"Well, I'm gonna go home and get some sleep," Grace said, yawning and stretching. "I was waiting by the phone all night to hear from you two!"

"Thanks, Grace," Nicky said. "I really appreciate all the work you've put in." Grace always proved to be a helpful ally in times of need. She wasn't there on the field, but she could quickly dig up information that sometimes got them out of a bind, and Nicky appreciated that.

"Of course." Grace winked. "Have fun, you two."

Nicky's face flushed. Once alone with Ken, she hesitantly locked eyes with him. They'd been through so much together now. Nicky felt closer to him, yet there was still a barrier that needed to be broken down even more. Maybe they could work on that together.

"So, uh..." He rubbed the back of his neck. "Any chance you want to get that drink tonight? It's probably gonna be our only chance to do it."

Nicky laughed, feeling light. He was right--this probably would be the only time, as they'd be back to work before they knew it. After so many losses--and victories--Nicky knew that even she needed some time off sometimes, to keep her mind healthy.

"Sure, Ken. Let's do it."

***

Later that night, Nicky found herself in a nice restaurant in downtown Jacksonville. Cool, blue lighting and a calm, soothing atmosphere permeated the restaurant from its tasteful surroundings. White tablecloths and blue-rimmed glassware accented the tables. Every table held a vase of fresh-cut roses and long, slender candles that flickered slightly in the cool breeze from the air conditioner.

Ken sat across from her in a booth, looking more relaxed than she was used to seeing him. An unbuttoned beige suit jacket with a dark purple shirt underneath, even leaving a button or two open, with his black hair holding some sort of product. He looked good.

Nicky cradled a glass of red wine, wearing a form-fitting brown dress, and her long brown hair in curls. She wasn't used to dressing up like this. But it felt right, somehow, to be here with Ken. It felt… normal. How much normal did they get to have in their lives? It was nice to kick back a little.

"So, tell me about Nicky Lyons before the FBI," Ken said.

Nicky took a sip of her wine, relishing in the acidity. "Oh, God, well, I guess I was a bit of a party animal when I lived in West Virginia."

Ken lifted a brow. "You? Really?"

"You can't see it?" Nicky asked, smirking.

"Oh, I can," Ken said. "But I never get to see you relaxed, so it's hard to picture you, well, kicking back and partying."

Nicky laughed. "Okay, well, I was kind of a wild card. I did what I wanted, when I wanted to." She twirled her wineglass in her hands, her mind going down a darker path. "But I changed when..." She trailed off, swallowing hard. She didn't want to think about Rosie right now. This was the one time, the one night, she was supposed to give herself off.

"Sorry." Ken cleared his throat. "I didn't mean to, uh, bring up the past..."

"It's fine." Nicky smiled. But for a moment, things felt a bit weird. They needed to talk about non-work-related things, but dark pasts didn't make great dinner conversation either.

"I'm sorry, I guess I'm not very good at this," Ken said, his cheeks red, which only endeared him to Nicky more. It was nice to see him so human.

Nicky laughed. "It's fine. I don't know what I'm doing either, if we're being honest. All I know how to talk about is work, and I'm trying really hard to not do that right now."

Nicky's hand was draped on the table. When Ken reached forward and touched it, she froze. His skin felt warm and callused on hers, and Nicky watched as he picked up her hand and placed a kiss on top of it, holding his lips there.

She was stunned. Stunned at how good it felt—and stunned that this relationship was really happening for her. It felt real, and Nicky had spent much of her life believing something like this just wasn’t for her.

"I like you for you, Lyons," he said. "If you wanna talk about work, to hell with it, let's talk about work. If you wanna talk about all the messed up shit that's happened in your past, then we can do that too. I'm just happy I'm here with you."

Something strange and foreign welled up in Nicky's heart. She was speechless. When Ken dropped her hand, she felt ten times colder. But the burn of attraction for him--it was growing. She felt something she hadn't had in a while--desire. To be close to him. To really know him, all of him, and for him to know her, too.

"I'm happy you're here, too," she said, her voice coming out lower than she expected. "But I'll pass on the work talk. Let me ask you something. Where do you want to be in five years?"

"Is this a job interview?" Ken asked, laughing.

"Of course, Walker," Nicky said. "I am your boss, after all." She shot him a wink, and his face flushed. He laughed and shook his head.

"Five years, I'd like to be my own boss. I'm thirty-five, not getting any younger. I'd like to get promoted to Special Agent, then move my way up the ladder. Maybe I could even be your boss for a change."

Nicky smiled at him. "You could be, if you play your cards right."

"That's the plan." Ken finished his wine. "Now it's your turn."

"You don't wanna know about that stuff," Nicky said, shaking her head. "Not really."

"I do."

Nicky took a breath. "Five years from now, I'd like... I'd like to have closure."

Ken blinked at her, then nodded. "Closure. Okay."

"On the Rosie case. I want to be able to move on. I don't want to be like everyone else. I want to be able to finally close the case, move on with my life, and know that she's okay. And even if she’s not okay… I need to know that, too. Closure, I guess that’s all I really want.”

Ken was silent for a moment. He reached across the table, taking her hand and squeezing it. "I think you can do it, you know. I know you can."

Nicky was silent. She wanted to believe him. She wanted to believe in herself. The past few months had been too much, and she had been exposed to too much—she felt closer than ever before, yet still so far away. But she had to keep trying, like she would for those missing girls.

Just then, Nicky's phone started buzzing in her purse beside her. "Ah, sorry, I thought I turned that thing on silent."

Ken gave her a look. "Go on, Lyons, I know you want to check it."

She bit her lip, feeling sorry. "Are you sure? We're--"

"Lyons. You forget how well I know you at this point. Answer the phone."

Nicky laughed. They really did feel like partners, in more ways than one. She fished her phone from her purse, expecting it to be work.

But it was the prison.

Nicky's breath caught. With all the chaos of the Harrison Smith case, she hadn't given much more thought to Felix Anderson and the man she'd asked to become an informant on him. Nicky had needed to focus on more pressing matters, and now she was trying to relax--but here was the prison, calling her. Maybe it was good news.

"Go ahead, take it," Ken said.

"Sorry. I'll make it up to you!" Nicky stood up.

"I'll take you up on that," Ken said with a laugh, spreading his arms on the back of the booth.

Nicky ran out of the restaurant and landed on the warm street of downtown Jacksonville. The salty ocean air filled her nostrils, mingling with the scents of restaurants, cars, and exhaust fumes. She could hear the sounds of honking horns and voices calling out to one another, but it was better than taking a private call in the middle of a restaurant.

Nicky quickly answered it. "This is Agent Lyons."

"Agent Lyons, this is Brad Barker from the Fillmore Institution," he said. "Do you have a moment?"

"Of course," Nicky said.

"Fred Garrison, one of our inmates, says he has news for you. He wants to talk."

"Right now?" Nicky's pulse had never been louder.

"Yes, ma'am. Is it a bad time?"

Nicky looked back into the restaurant, where she saw Ken sitting there, waiting for her. She bit her lip. She could put this aside for one night, go in there and continue her date…

Or she could seize the chance for answers. If Ken really did care about her and understand her, then she knew he'd understand this, and how important this was to her.

"Now's perfect. Put him on."

NOW AVAILABLE!

ALL FOR ME
(A Nicky Lyons FBI Suspense Thriller—Book 7)

FBI Special Agent Nicky Lyons is stunned when a cassette tape arrives in the mail, blasting a killer's voice, taunting her to stop him from taking his next victim. In this killer's diabolical game of cat and mouse, Nicky must ask herself: is she one step ahead of him? Or a useful pawn for his game?

"A masterpiece of thriller and mystery."
—Books and Movie Reviews, Roberto Mattos (re Once Gone)

ALL FOR ME (A Nicky Lyons FBI Suspense Thriller) is book #7 in a long-anticipated new series by #1 bestseller and USA Today bestselling author Blake Pierce, whose bestseller Once Gone (a free download) has received over 7,000 five star ratings and reviews.

A page-turning and harrowing crime thriller featuring a brilliant and tortured FBI agent, the NICKY LYONS series is a riveting mystery, packed with non-stop action, suspense, twists and turns, revelations, and driven by a breakneck pace that will keep you flipping pages late into the night. Fans of Rachel Caine, Teresa Driscoll and Robert Dugoni are sure to fall in love.

Future books in the series will soon be available.

"An edge of your seat thriller in a new series that keeps you turning pages! ...So many twists, turns and red herrings… I can't wait to see what happens next."
—Reader review (Her Last Wish)

"A strong, complex story about two FBI agents trying to stop a serial killer. If you want an author to capture your attention and have you guessing, yet trying to put the pieces together, Pierce is your author!"
—Reader review (Her Last Wish)

"A typical Blake Pierce twisting, turning, roller coaster ride suspense thriller. Will have you turning the pages to the last sentence of the last chapter!!!"
—Reader review (City of Prey)

"Right from the start we have an unusual protagonist that I haven't seen done in this genre before. The action is nonstop… A very atmospheric novel that will keep you turning pages well into the wee hours."
—Reader review (City of Prey)

"Everything that I look for in a book… a great plot, interesting characters, and grabs your interest right away. The book moves along at a breakneck pace and stays that way until the end. Now on go I to book two!"
—Reader review (Girl, Alone)

"Exciting, heart pounding, edge of your seat book… a must read for mystery and suspense readers!"
—Reader review (Girl, Alone)

Blake Pierce

Blake Pierce is the USA Today bestselling author of the RILEY PAGE mystery series, which includes seventeen books. Blake Pierce is also the author of the MACKENZIE WHITE mystery series, comprising fourteen books; of the AVERY BLACK mystery series, comprising six books; of the KERI LOCKE mystery series, comprising five books; of the MAKING OF RILEY PAIGE mystery series, comprising six books; of the KATE WISE mystery series, comprising seven books; of the CHLOE FINE psychological suspense mystery, comprising six books; of the JESSIE HUNT psychological suspense thriller series, comprising twenty six books; of the AU PAIR psychological suspense thriller series, comprising three books; of the ZOE PRIME mystery series, comprising six books; of the ADELE SHARP mystery series, comprising sixteen books, of the EUROPEAN VOYAGE cozy mystery series, comprising six books; of the LAURA FROST FBI suspense thriller, comprising eleven books; of the ELLA DARK FBI suspense thriller, comprising fourteen books (and counting); of the A YEAR IN EUROPE cozy mystery series, comprising nine books, of the AVA GOLD mystery series, comprising six books; of the RACHEL GIFT mystery series, comprising ten books (and counting); of the VALERIE LAW mystery series, comprising nine books (and counting); of the PAIGE KING mystery series, comprising eight books (and counting); of the MAY MOORE mystery series, comprising eleven books (and counting); the CORA SHIELDS mystery series, comprising five books (and counting); of the NICKY LYONS mystery series, comprising seven books (and counting), of the CAMI LARK mystery series, comprising five books (and counting), of the AMBER YOUNG mystery series, comprising five books (and counting), of the DAISY FORTUNE mystery series, comprising five books (and counting), and of the new FIONA RED mystery series, comprising five books (and counting).

An avid reader and lifelong fan of the mystery and thriller genres, Blake loves to hear from you, so please feel free to visit www.blakepierceauthor.com to learn more and stay in touch.

BOOKS BY BLAKE PIERCE

FIONA RED MYSTERY SERIES
LET HER GO (Book #1)
LET HER BE (Book #2)
LET HER HOPE (Book #3)
LET HER WISH (Book #4)
LET HER LIVE (Book #5)

DAISY FORTUNE MYSTERY SERIES
NEED YOU (Book #1)
CLAIM YOU (Book #2)
CRAVE YOU (Book #3)
CHOOSE YOU (Book #4)
CHASE YOU (Book #5)

AMBER YOUNG MYSTERY SERIES
ABSENT PITY (Book #1)
ABSENT REMORSE (Book #2)
ABSENT FEELING (Book #3)
ABSENT MERCY (Book #4)
ABSENT REASON (Book #5)

CAMI LARK MYSTERY SERIES
JUST ME (Book #1)
JUST OUTSIDE (Book #2)
JUST RIGHT (Book #3)
JUST FORGET (Book #4)
JUST ONCE (Book #5)

NICKY LYONS MYSTERY SERIES
ALL MINE (Book #1)
ALL HIS (Book #2)
ALL HE SEES (Book #3)
ALL ALONE (Book #4)
ALL FOR ONE (Book #5)
ALL HE TAKES (Book #6)
ALL FOR ME (Book #7)

CORA SHIELDS MYSTERY SERIES

UNDONE (Book #1)
UNWANTED (Book #2)
UNHINGED (Book #3)
UNSAID (Book #4)
UNGLUED (Book #5)

MAY MOORE SUSPENSE THRILLER

NEVER RUN (Book #1)
NEVER TELL (Book #2)
NEVER LIVE (Book #3)
NEVER HIDE (Book #4)
NEVER FORGIVE (Book #5)
NEVER AGAIN (Book #6)
NEVER LOOK BACK (Book #7)
NEVER FORGET (Book #8)
NEVER LET GO (Book #9)
NEVER PRETEND (Book #10)
NEVER HESITATE (Book #11)

PAIGE KING MYSTERY SERIES

THE GIRL HE PINED (Book #1)
THE GIRL HE CHOSE (Book #2)
THE GIRL HE TOOK (Book #3)
THE GIRL HE WISHED (Book #4)
THE GIRL HE CROWNED (Book #5)
THE GIRL HE WATCHED (Book #6)
THE GIRL HE WANTED (Book #7)
THE GIRL HE CLAIMED (Book #8)

VALERIE LAW MYSTERY SERIES

NO MERCY (Book #1)
NO PITY (Book #2)
NO FEAR (Book #3)
NO SLEEP (Book #4)
NO QUARTER (Book #5)
NO CHANCE (Book #6)
NO REFUGE (Book #7)
NO GRACE (Book #8)
NO ESCAPE (Book #9)

RACHEL GIFT MYSTERY SERIES
HER LAST WISH (Book #1)
HER LAST CHANCE (Book #2)
HER LAST HOPE (Book #3)
HER LAST FEAR (Book #4)
HER LAST CHOICE (Book #5)
HER LAST BREATH (Book #6)
HER LAST MISTAKE (Book #7)
HER LAST DESIRE (Book #8)
HER LAST REGRET (Book #9)
HER LAST HOUR (Book #10)

AVA GOLD MYSTERY SERIES
CITY OF PREY (Book #1)
CITY OF FEAR (Book #2)
CITY OF BONES (Book #3)
CITY OF GHOSTS (Book #4)
CITY OF DEATH (Book #5)
CITY OF VICE (Book #6)

A YEAR IN EUROPE
A MURDER IN PARIS (Book #1)
DEATH IN FLORENCE (Book #2)
VENGEANCE IN VIENNA (Book #3)
A FATALITY IN SPAIN (Book #4)

ELLA DARK FBI SUSPENSE THRILLER
GIRL, ALONE (Book #1)
GIRL, TAKEN (Book #2)
GIRL, HUNTED (Book #3)
GIRL, SILENCED (Book #4)
GIRL, VANISHED (Book 5)
GIRL ERASED (Book #6)
GIRL, FORSAKEN (Book #7)
GIRL, TRAPPED (Book #8)
GIRL, EXPENDABLE (Book #9)
GIRL, ESCAPED (Book #10)
GIRL, HIS (Book #11)
GIRL, LURED (Book #12)
GIRL, MISSING (Book #13)
GIRL, UNKNOWN (Book #14)

LAURA FROST FBI SUSPENSE THRILLER
ALREADY GONE (Book #1)
ALREADY SEEN (Book #2)
ALREADY TRAPPED (Book #3)
ALREADY MISSING (Book #4)
ALREADY DEAD (Book #5)
ALREADY TAKEN (Book #6)
ALREADY CHOSEN (Book #7)
ALREADY LOST (Book #8)
ALREADY HIS (Book #9)
ALREADY LURED (Book #10)
ALREADY COLD (Book #11)

EUROPEAN VOYAGE COZY MYSTERY SERIES
MURDER (AND BAKLAVA) (Book #1)
DEATH (AND APPLE STRUDEL) (Book #2)
CRIME (AND LAGER) (Book #3)
MISFORTUNE (AND GOUDA) (Book #4)
CALAMITY (AND A DANISH) (Book #5)
MAYHEM (AND HERRING) (Book #6)

ADELE SHARP MYSTERY SERIES
LEFT TO DIE (Book #1)
LEFT TO RUN (Book #2)
LEFT TO HIDE (Book #3)
LEFT TO KILL (Book #4)
LEFT TO MURDER (Book #5)
LEFT TO ENVY (Book #6)
LEFT TO LAPSE (Book #7)
LEFT TO VANISH (Book #8)
LEFT TO HUNT (Book #9)
LEFT TO FEAR (Book #10)
LEFT TO PREY (Book #11)
LEFT TO LURE (Book #12)
LEFT TO CRAVE (Book #13)
LEFT TO LOATHE (Book #14)
LEFT TO HARM (Book #15)
LEFT TO RUIN (Book #16)

THE AU PAIR SERIES

ALMOST GONE (Book#1)
ALMOST LOST (Book #2)
ALMOST DEAD (Book #3)

ZOE PRIME MYSTERY SERIES
FACE OF DEATH (Book#1)
FACE OF MURDER (Book #2)
FACE OF FEAR (Book #3)
FACE OF MADNESS (Book #4)
FACE OF FURY (Book #5)
FACE OF DARKNESS (Book #6)

A JESSIE HUNT PSYCHOLOGICAL SUSPENSE SERIES
THE PERFECT WIFE (Book #1)
THE PERFECT BLOCK (Book #2)
THE PERFECT HOUSE (Book #3)
THE PERFECT SMILE (Book #4)
THE PERFECT LIE (Book #5)
THE PERFECT LOOK (Book #6)
THE PERFECT AFFAIR (Book #7)
THE PERFECT ALIBI (Book #8)
THE PERFECT NEIGHBOR (Book #9)
THE PERFECT DISGUISE (Book #10)
THE PERFECT SECRET (Book #11)
THE PERFECT FAÇADE (Book #12)
THE PERFECT IMPRESSION (Book #13)
THE PERFECT DECEIT (Book #14)
THE PERFECT MISTRESS (Book #15)
THE PERFECT IMAGE (Book #16)
THE PERFECT VEIL (Book #17)
THE PERFECT INDISCRETION (Book #18)
THE PERFECT RUMOR (Book #19)
THE PERFECT COUPLE (Book #20)
THE PERFECT MURDER (Book #21)
THE PERFECT HUSBAND (Book #22)
THE PERFECT SCANDAL (Book #23)
THE PERFECT MASK (Book #24)
THE PERFECT RUSE (Book #25)
THE PERFECT VENEER (Book #26)

CHLOE FINE PSYCHOLOGICAL SUSPENSE SERIES

NEXT DOOR (Book #1)
A NEIGHBOR'S LIE (Book #2)
CUL DE SAC (Book #3)
SILENT NEIGHBOR (Book #4)
HOMECOMING (Book #5)
TINTED WINDOWS (Book #6)

KATE WISE MYSTERY SERIES
IF SHE KNEW (Book #1)
IF SHE SAW (Book #2)
IF SHE RAN (Book #3)
IF SHE HID (Book #4)
IF SHE FLED (Book #5)
IF SHE FEARED (Book #6)
IF SHE HEARD (Book #7)

THE MAKING OF RILEY PAIGE SERIES
WATCHING (Book #1)
WAITING (Book #2)
LURING (Book #3)
TAKING (Book #4)
STALKING (Book #5)
KILLING (Book #6)

RILEY PAIGE MYSTERY SERIES
ONCE GONE (Book #1)
ONCE TAKEN (Book #2)
ONCE CRAVED (Book #3)
ONCE LURED (Book #4)
ONCE HUNTED (Book #5)
ONCE PINED (Book #6)
ONCE FORSAKEN (Book #7)
ONCE COLD (Book #8)
ONCE STALKED (Book #9)
ONCE LOST (Book #10)
ONCE BURIED (Book #11)
ONCE BOUND (Book #12)
ONCE TRAPPED (Book #13)
ONCE DORMANT (Book #14)
ONCE SHUNNED (Book #15)
ONCE MISSED (Book #16)

ONCE CHOSEN (Book #17)

MACKENZIE WHITE MYSTERY SERIES
BEFORE HE KILLS (Book #1)
BEFORE HE SEES (Book #2)
BEFORE HE COVETS (Book #3)
BEFORE HE TAKES (Book #4)
BEFORE HE NEEDS (Book #5)
BEFORE HE FEELS (Book #6)
BEFORE HE SINS (Book #7)
BEFORE HE HUNTS (Book #8)
BEFORE HE PREYS (Book #9)
BEFORE HE LONGS (Book #10)
BEFORE HE LAPSES (Book #11)
BEFORE HE ENVIES (Book #12)
BEFORE HE STALKS (Book #13)
BEFORE HE HARMS (Book #14)

AVERY BLACK MYSTERY SERIES
CAUSE TO KILL (Book #1)
CAUSE TO RUN (Book #2)
CAUSE TO HIDE (Book #3)
CAUSE TO FEAR (Book #4)
CAUSE TO SAVE (Book #5)
CAUSE TO DREAD (Book #6)

KERI LOCKE MYSTERY SERIES
A TRACE OF DEATH (Book #1)
A TRACE OF MURDER (Book #2)
A TRACE OF VICE (Book #3)
A TRACE OF CRIME (Book #4)
A TRACE OF HOPE (Book #5)

Made in United States
Troutdale, OR
02/14/2025

28972387R00096